DEAR NOBODY

BERLIE DOHERTY

Resource Material
Rachel O'Neill

Series Consultant
Cecily O'Neill

Collins Educational
An Imprint of HarperCollins*Publishers*

Published by Collins Educational, an imprint of HarperCollinsPublishers Ltd,
77–85 Fulham Palace Road, London W6 8JB

| www.**Collins**Education.com |
| On-line support for schools and colleges |

© Copyright 1995 Berlie Doherty and Rachel O'Neill

First published 1995 by Collins Educational

20 19 18 17 16 15 14 13 12 11

ISBN-13 978 0 00 320004 1
ISBN-10 0 00 320004 3

British Library Cataloguing in Publication Data

A catalogue record for this book is available from the British Library.

Design by Wendi Watson
Cover design by Chi Leung
Cover image: © Julie Toy/Getty Images/Stone
Typeset by Harper Phototypesetters Ltd, Northampton.
Printed and bound in China by Imago

Acknowledgements
The following permissions to reproduce material are gratefully acknowledged:

Illustrations: Nicola Cornish, p 75; Hulton Deutsch, p 77, 84; Gay Galsworthy,
pp 60, 61, 71, 87, 92; Mark Kensett, pp 67, 70; Photofusion, p 73.
Text extracts: From Dear Nobody (the novel) by Berlie Doherty, Hamish Hamilton
1991, pp 67–69; from Autobiography by Louis MacNeice, Faber & Faber 1982,
p 72; Workhouse to the Workplace, NCOPF, pp 73, 83; The Guardian p 77; The
Sunday Times pp 79–80; From The Common Thread by Kitty Fitzgerald, Mandarin,
pp 81–82; from A Taste of Honey by Shelagh Delaney pp 88–93; The Lullaby by
Richard Jones, Virago 1993 p 94; Pregnant Teenager on the Beach by Mary Balazs,
Virago 1993, p 94; My Baby Has No Name Yet by Kim Nam-Jo, Virago 1993, p 95.

Whilst every effort has been made both to contact the copyright holders, this has
not proved possible in every case.

Commissioning Editor: Domenica de Rosa
Editors: Rebecca Lloyd and Sara Fielding
Production by James Graves

For permission to perform this play, please allow plenty of time and contact:
Permissions Department, HarperCollinsPublishers,
77–85 Fulham Palace Road, London W6 8JB. Tel. 0208 307 4303.

CONTENTS

BACKGROUND TO THE PLAY

Dear Nobody was first a novel. I set myself quite a challenge in writing it. Essentially it's a story about love, but that doesn't mean it's a 'love story' in the romantic sense. It is about two young people who love each other, but it's also about family love - the ways in which love can go wrong, how love sometimes makes us do things that aren't sensible, or that hurt people, how love sometimes turns to hate and drives people and families apart.

In the story, when Helen finds out that she is pregnant, she feels she has no one to turn to. She daren't tell her mother. She daren't tell Chris, because parenthood is not something they have ever contemplated - they're too young for that. She feels utterly alone, and gives voice to the fear inside herself by writing letters to her unborn child, whom she calls 'Nobody'.

But it isn't just Helen's story. Chris finds that, long before he is ready for parenthood, he is to become a father. If anything *his* sense of shock and fear is greater than Helen's, because he is powerless to make any choices about it.

And then they have to face their families. Even though they feel terribly alone with their dilemma, they can't keep it a secret forever. Everything we do affects somebody else, often in a surprising way. *Dear Nobody* is not just about the journey that Helen and Chris make towards becoming parents. It is also about getting to know their own parents properly.

I talked to lots of young people in schools when I was writing the novel. I didn't want to write about their experiences because I had the story and characters in my head by then. But I did not know how people of your age feel about love and friendship, relationships with parents, responsibility and loyalty. Since I wrote the novel it has been published in many different languages all round the world, and in several different forms, including this play for schools. I think maybe the reason why it has had such a wide appeal is because the subject that it deals with - love, and all its complications - is something that effects us all in one way or another, and *that* really matters to us. Sometimes it is embarrassing to talk about love - whether it's physical or emotional - and a play and a story can help us to understand things that are difficult to handle.

That's why I felt I was setting myself a challenge when I wrote *Dear Nobody*. I wanted to look at this important subject of love in a way that matters to boys and to girls, and to their parents as well. I hope it works for you.

Berlie Doherty

THE CHARACTERS

HELEN GARTON – a seventeen-year-old girl
CHRIS MARSHALL – an eighteen-year-old boy
ALICE GARTON – Helen's mother
TED GARTON – Helen's father
ALAN MARSHALL – Chris's father
JOAN – Chris's mother
DON – Joan's partner
RUTHLYN – Helen's friend, aged seventeen
TOM – Chris's friend, aged seventeen
NAN – Helen's grandmother
GRANDAD – Helen's grandfather
BRYN – an eighteen-year-old girl
MR HARRINGTON – Chris and Tom's English teacher
DOCTOR
NURSE
MALE SHOP ASSISTANT

The following parts were doubled up in the original
production of the play at the Crucible Theatre, Sheffield,
1993:

ALICE and **BRYN**
NAN, JOAN, RUTHLYN and **NURSE**
TOM and **TED**
ALAN, SHOP ASSISTANT, DON, MR HARRINGTON

First performed at the Crucible Theatre, Sheffield, in 1993,
Dear Nobody won the 1994 Writer's Guild/Wimpey award for
best children's drama.

DEAR NOBODY

ACT ONE

*The acting area is arranged so that two scenes can take place at the same time. There will be a central, neutral acting area, and in addition, **Helen's** bedroom will be at one raised end of the set, **Chris's** at the other.*

*Chris and **Helen** enter. They are both about 18. **Helen** goes to her bed, **Chris**, to his chair. Both are writing. Gradually **Chris** looks up and begins to address the audience.*

CHRIS Maybe we all want to burn off across the horizon, – into space, perhaps, – to take off into some unknown territory and meet ourselves out there. It is late Autumn, and this is where I begin to write, where I open a door into the past. It leads into a room in my own house, in a back street not far from the city centre. From my window I can see the lights of thousands of houses that dot out the contours of the hills and valleys of Sheffield.

This is the story of a journey. It took me away from Sheffield and away from my dad. I suppose it took me away from my childhood.

HELEN *writing* November. Dear Chris, I think I'm exactly where I want to be, at this moment of my life. I think of you often. I hope you're happy too.

CHRIS It's Helen's journey too. Nobody ever travels on their own.

It all began last January, on a dark evening that was full of snow. That's where this journey really begins.

*He looks towards **Helen**.*

Funny, we were just kids then. Ten months ago.

*Ruthlyn and **Tom** run on to centre stage. It is winter and it* *is snowing. They are high and excited, throwing snowballs at each other. They, too, are about 18, but are responding in a very skittish way to the snow, shoving it down each other's necks, etc.*

HELEN   Oh, great, it's snowing!

Helen and Chris run and meet up and run hand in hand to join Ruthlyn and Tom. Tom is giving Ruthlyn a hard time.

RUTHLYN   *half-laughing, half-angry*   Oh give over, Tom. I'm soaked through. I said give over, will you!

CHRIS   Get him, Ruthlyn! Kill!

All three pelt Tom with snowballs.

TOM   *laughing*   Chris, you moron, whose side are you on, anyway?

Tom subsides, laughing, under a welter of snowball attack. Ruthlyn sits on him and finishes the job off by stuffing snow down his collar and trousers. Helen is jumping up and down, clapping in childish excitement. Chris watches her. He draws her to him and, in the middle of the hilarity, becomes very serious.

CHRIS   I love you, Nell.

HELEN   I love you.

RUTHLYN   Time to go, Tom. I think these two want to be alone together.

TOM   I'll get you for this, Marshall. Return match after school tomorrow, right?

Chris and Helen are so absorbed in each other that they hear nothing of this. Tom and Ruthlyn laugh.

RUTHLYN   We're off now!

TOM   See you both!

He chucks a parting snowball at Chris and is ignored. Chris and Helen are standing with their arms around each other. They break away a little to walk home together.

CHRIS   I hate the thought of October already. I wish I'd never applied to Newcastle now. Newcastle, and you'll be in Manchester! They're miles away from each other!

HELEN   October's miles away as well, Chris. It's ten months off! Don't get sad yet. Let's make the most of being together now.

They enter Helen's house and look round, expecting to find her parents there.

HELEN I'm home!

There's nobody in, Chris.

He puts his arms round her and lights dim as they go to her room and loud music comes on. We see them embrace and lie down.

Darkness and music, no other sounds, broken into by the sound of a car on the gravel and the sweep of headlights. Music over.

HELEN It's them, Chris!

CHRIS Oh, God.

They make a mess of trying to straighten up the sheet and themselves, laughing at the fun of it.

*Lights as **Helen's** parents come in, carrying supermarket bags. **Alice** is a fussy, rather cold woman in early middle-age. **Ted** is shy and easily embarrassed, a lover of music. Can often be heard humming pieces of classical music (Bach) or jazz, practising keyboard runs on table-tops, etc, not really taking part in conversations.*

ALICE Helen! Come and give us a hand! Where is the girl?

TED Pom-de-pom, pom-tom-te-tom!

*Humming, not listening, he bumbles round until he finds the piano, where he sits and, as if by habit, begins to play. **Alice** is exasperated.*

ALICE Oh, you're useless! Helen!

Helen tumbles in, looking flushed and dishevelled.

HELEN Oh, hello Mum. I didn't hear you coming in.

ALICE I didn't think you could be out, not on a weekday.

HELEN I was doing some work in my room.

ALICE You knew we'd have stuff to carry in.

Chris enters, looking self-conscious.

CHRIS Hello, Mrs Garton.

TED *pleased* Hello, Chris! How's the guitar coming on?

CHRIS Okay, thanks. Helen's been teaching me some new chords.

TED That's good. That's good.

ALICE I'd like to know what Chris is doing here on a weekday, Helen, and why he was up in your room.

Ted bangs at the piano, embarrassed.

HELEN Mum! We've just come in, if you must know. I was

doing some work at Ruthlyn's, and Chris and Tom came round. Chris walked me home.

ALICE He doesn't have to walk you all the way upstairs, young lady.

TED Did you write your letter, Helen?

HELEN Oh Dad! I forgot!

TED You forgot?

ALICE What's she done now?

TED She's only forgotten the most important letter of her life, that's all.

HELEN It doesn't matter, Dad. I can do it now.

TED Her acceptance to the Manchester Royal College of Music, that's all.

*It is clear from **Ted's** attitude that he is not only personally disappointed but that he holds **Chris** to blame.*

CHRIS I'd better go.

ALICE I think you had.

HELEN I'll see you out, Chris.

*While **Helen** and **Chris** move to the door area **Alice** continues to unpack goods and **Ted** sits again at the piano.*

CHRIS I'm sorry.

HELEN Don't be. It matters so much to Dad. Nearly as much as it matters to me. But it'll be all right. There's still time to accept. And don't mind Mum. It's nothing to do with you – she's just like that.

CHRIS I love you, Nell.

ALICE Helen, shut that door! It's like a fridge in here!

CHRIS I want it to happen all over again.

HELEN There'll be lots more times.

CHRIS Promise?

HELEN Promise.

*Chris back-dances off, waving, and watched by **Helen**. As she goes back to the room **Alice** goes off stage and **Helen**, still bubbly in spite of her father's disappointment, sits at the piano next to him. They begin to play a duet together, laughing. It is obvious they are very close. **Alice** enters and watches, left out, and goes.*

*Chris's house. **Alan** comes on and switches on the television, sits down to watch it.*

He has a slight limp. About fifty, he is a home-loving man who has brought up his son. He has a very good relationship with **Chris**.

Ted *and* **Helen** *freeze, lights down on them, as* **Chris** *comes in. He too is very bubbly at first.*

CHRIS   Hi Dad.

ALAN   Hello Chris. Had your tea?

CHRIS   I'm not hungry.

He picks up his guitar and starts strumming it, composing a song for **Helen**. *His guitar playing is very basic.*

CHRIS   *singing*   This is my *pause for change of guitar chord*   song *pause for change of guitar chord*   for you *pause for change of guitar   chord*   love.

Stops and starts again several times.

ALAN   *amused*   Not feeling too good?

CHRIS   *singing*   This is my . . .
This is my song for you *pause for change of guitar chord*
love
You have wound yourself around my mind
You are part of my *pause for guitar chord*   heart . . .

ALAN   For goodness sake, Chris! Pack it in now. Give the cat some peace.

CHRIS   *singing, falteringly*   This is my song for you *pause* love
You walk *pause* through my waking dreams
Like the *pause* ghost of sleep.

ALAN   I was trying to watch a film.

Chris *puts down the guitar. At this point he is coltishly cheerful.*

CHRIS   You shouldn't be watching this. It's rude.

ALAN   I close my eyes when the naughty bits come on.

CHRIS   Dad?

ALAN   Mmm?

CHRIS   What happened to you and Mum?

ALAN   You know what happened. She walked out.

CHRIS   I mean, why?

ALAN   She met a fella, didn't she, and he was younger than me with a bit more hair on top and he wore natty jumpers and he read a lot of books. She decided she liked him better than me and off she went. I came home one night and I'd done a shift – I was dead tired, you know – and there she was standing in the hall with her coat on and this fella was with her. And she told me she was leaving.

CHRIS Did you know him?

*At this stage we get the feeling that **Chris** has blundered in deeper than he ever intended, and that **Alan** is opening up a wound that has long been covered up. Once he starts he can't stop, but **Chris** becomes uncomfortable and embarrassed.*

ALAN As a matter of fact, I did. Not well, of course. But he'd been round a couple of times. Some climber or other. Didn't suspect a thing. That's what your mother hated most about me, of course. She said I'd got no imagination. Funny, I didn't know how much I loved your mother till she told me she was leaving me. You'd think I would have hated her. I did later. No one likes to be rejected, you know. I hated her because she didn't want me. And I hated her because she was splitting up a family. I didn't want that to happen, and I was powerless to stop it. How old were you then?

CHRIS Ten.

ALAN You see. There you were – 'Where's Mum?' 'Where's Mum?' every five minutes. How could I explain to you that she wasn't coming back? So it helped, being able to hate her.

But I'll tell you something else, Chris, and this'll shock you a bit. I used to wish that she was dead. If she'd died, you see, I could have got it over with. There are ways of dealing with death. There are funerals and flowers and crying. It would have been terrible, but I would have known absolutely certainly that she wasn't going to come back and that I was never, ever going to see her again, and somehow I'd have got on with my life and with you. But while someone's alive there's always a chance that they'll come back again, so you can never quite let go. I wanted her back, however much I hated her for going.

Chris would like to leave, or to ask his father to stop, but Alan is almost talking to himself now.

ALAN I used to think of her enjoying herself with this natty bloke with all his books. And I knew that she couldn't be happy. Not really. I knew she'd be going through hell. Don't tell me any woman can walk away from

her own kid and carry on as if nothing had happened.
I think she went through hell.

CHRIS   Why didn't you get married again or something?

ALAN   Ouch!

*Chris sees how insensitive he has been, but can't help saying what he wanted to say. He comes close to **Alan** and tries to say it gently.*

CHRIS   I just wondered, Dad, you don't happen to have Mum's address, do you?

ALAN   I should have. Somewhere. Why?

CHRIS   I was thinking I might go and see her sometime.

*Chris goes to his room. **Alan,** obviously distressed, sits staring into space, locked in memories. **Chris** is aware of this. He takes out a file pad and a pen and starts to write.*

CHRIS   Dear Mum. You'll be surprised to hear from me.

*Alan and **Ted** leave the stage. **Chris** approaches the central area and is joined by **Helen.***

HELEN   Are you sure you're doing the right thing, writing to her like this? I don't want you to get hurt, Chris.

CHRIS   Why should I get hurt?

HELEN   You won't bring her back, you know. Not after all this time.

CHRIS   I don't want to bring her back. I want to meet her again, that's all. I just want to believe in her.

Helen goes.

CHRIS   *to himself*   I'm nothing to my mother, after all. I'm a speck of dust, and I've blown away.

Joan, his mother, appears at side of stage, reading the letter. Lights off.

*Lights up on **Helen,** putting on her coat.*

ALICE   *enters*   You off to school? You haven't had your breakfast.

HELEN   I don't feel like any this morning, Mum. I've got a bit of a head-ache. I'll be a bit late tonight. I thought I'd go round and see Nan on my way home. I haven't seen her and Grandad for ages.

ALICE   I don't want you walking home in the dark.

HELEN   Why don't you come? You never go to see Nan.

ALICE   I don't want to, that's why.

Helen looks at her oddly. This is a subject which is often raised, never explained, and which hurts them both.

HELEN *leaving* I'll give her your love, then.

She goes, with schoolbag.

Alice, tight-lipped, goes off in the opposite direction

*Chris enters, with his schoolbag and an unopened letter. He looks at the post-mark, pleased, and tears it open. He leaves the house, reading the letter, and is overtaken by **Tom**, who snatches it off him.*

CHRIS Hey, you berk, give it back!

TOM Chrissy's got a love letter. Darling, darling . . . *Waves it in the air, teasing **Chris**. **Chris** is genuinely angry, rugby tackles **Tom** who is bigger and stronger and easily holds him back.*

CHRIS I'm telling you, Tom, I'll kill you if you damage that letter. I've waited a month for it.

*Tom blows kisses at him and, recognising at last that **Chris** is not to be teased, drops the letter. He runs off, and **Chris**, picking up the letter, runs after him.*

Nan enters and sits on stage. Although she is only in her early seventies she is frail and withdrawn, a woman who has aged before her time and has little interest in life. She stares out of her window, locked in her thoughts.

*Grandad enters with **Helen**. **Nan** just about registers her and looks away again.*

GRANDAD Look who's come to see us, Dorrie. It's our little Helen.

NAN She's not so little.

*She stares at **Helen**, as if she knows something about her. **Helen** is uncomfortable. They sit in silence.*

HELEN What do you think about all day, Nan?

NAN Think about? What is there to think about?

HELEN Are you remembering your childhood?

NAN When I was a child I lived in a drawer.

HELEN In a drawer, Nan?

NAN I lived in a drawer. In them days, if you couldn't afford cradle nor cot, you put your bairns in a drawer. Good enough, I'd say. And anyway, what better place to hide me, eh? If I cried too much, or if the lady from upstairs wanted to visit the kitchens, my mother just had to push the drawer, and I'd disappear. Very handy, if you think about it.

HELEN   But she didn't do it, Nan, did she?

NAN   It wasn't that she wasn't married, if that's what you're thinking. She was married to the butler. But she wasn't allowed to have a child, you see, not while she was in service. She'd have lost her job. So I was a secret.

HELEN   But she didn't close the drawer?

NAN   I believe I can remember it now. Shelves right up there, stacked with black pots. I can hear the sounds of skirts and footsteps and voices. I can remember daylight changing into dark across my face, like that. I can remember sliding, and a sudden jolting. Crack! And I can smell it too, stuffy and sweet.

HELEN   Weren't you frightened?

NAN   Too young to be frightened. Besides, I like the dark.

Grandad, Nan and Helen go.

Chris, night-time, moorland. He is in waterproof gear and it is cold and wet. He stands with hands in pockets, obviously waiting for Helen to catch up. As she comes on, in wet waterproofs, he holds out his hand for her, but she doesn't take it. She is obviously fed up.

CHRIS   Thanks for coming, Helen. I needed to see you.

HELEN   I must be mad. It's the coldest night of the year and we have to come out on Stanage Edge of all places!

CHRIS   My mum used to bring me here, when I was a kid. Imagine seeing the dawn from up here! Why don't we do that one night? We could bring a tent, Helen, and we could watch the sun go down, and see the moon and stars coming out, and the next day we'd watch the dawn . . .

HELEN   *is taken up with his enthusiasm*   And then we'd stagger into school for registration and tell my mum that we'd missed the last bus home.

CHRIS   We could come in June. We could just sleep out in the heather – we wouldn't need a tent then. There'd just be us . . .

HELEN   And a few sheep nibbling at us.

CHRIS   We could come on the longest day. There's a cave along the edge – we could sleep in there.

HELEN   *changing mood abruptly* Meanwhile, let's go home. I'm famished. Actually, I feel sick, I'm so hungry. What was it you wanted to tell me, anyway? Let's get it over with.

Chris hands Helen the letter.

HELEN   What is it?

CHRIS   Read it. It's from my mother.

HELEN   I can't see in the dark, dope.

CHRIS   It says, 'Dear Christopher'. . .

HELEN   'Christopher'! That's a bit formal.

Joan appears, lit, at side of stage, while Chris recites the letter off by heart.

CHRIS   Thank you for your letter. It was a great surprise. I'm sorry I didn't reply straight away but I've only just returned from the Alps.

JOAN   Did you know that I'm now a professional photographer? I've been working on a commission to illustrate a mountaineering book. I climb too, of course, with Don.

Don joins Joan and puts his arm round her.

JOAN   This has been a wonderful job for me, and is going to take up several more months, I should think.

CHRIS   Yes, do come and see me. It would be lovely. With best wishes, Joan.

Joan and Don go

HELEN   'Joan'!

CHRIS   What else could she have put? With love from Mummy? I've been looking forward to showing you this all day. What d'you think?

HELEN   I don't like her.

CHRIS   You've never even met her.

HELEN   I don't like the way she calls you 'Christopher', for a start. What's wrong with Chris? Christopher's so formal, as if she's never met you in her life. And then she goes and calls herself 'Joan' at the end.

CHRIS   I thought that was brilliant. It's a way of saying, our relationship is different now, let's be friends.

HELEN   Great! I'll just disappear for eight years while you're an annoying brat and let's be friends now you've grown up.

CHRIS   Anything else you don't like about her, while you're at it?

HELEN   I don't like the way she goes on and on about

being a photographer and a climber and having commissions and all that.

CHRIS She doesn't go on and on.

HELEN She sounds like a show-off. She hasn't said a thing about you. How are your 'A' levels going? How's your dad? Have you still got the cat? All she's interested in is herself.

CHRIS 'Oh my dear Lady Disdain'.

HELEN She makes a point of saying she hasn't got time to see you.

CHRIS All right, all right.

HELEN You asked me. I'm only telling you because you asked me.

CHRIS I wish I hadn't shown it to you now.

HELEN I don't think you should try to see her, Chris. You'll get hurt. I've thought that all along.

CHRIS That's my business, isn't it? What's up with you these days?

HELEN Nothing.

CHRIS I seem to be upsetting you for some reason.

HELEN Nobody's upsetting me. Just go home or something. Don't keep on at me. It's not you. I started the day wrong. I shouldn't have come out, but we said tonight, so I came.

CHRIS *ironic* Thank you.

HELEN I'm going home. You don't have to come with me.

Chris is hurt. Music denotes the beginnings of anxiety and anguish.

Helen's house. He follows her in. Angry with each other, they toss down their coats and sit apart, not speaking.

CHRIS Talk to me, Helen.

HELEN I don't feel like talking.

CHRIS I'll do you some beans if you like.

HELEN I'm not hungry.

CHRIS All right. I'll make you some coffee.

HELEN I don't like coffee.

CHRIS First I've heard! You drink it by the gallon!

ALICE *comes in* What's up with you two? Had a tiff?

CHRIS Not as far as I know, Mrs Garton . . .

ALICE Looks to me as if you have. I'm always having tiffs with Ted, and he never seems to notice either. Men! Insensitive bunch! I think you're sickening for something, Helen. Your eyes are watery. You might be in for a dose of flu.

HELEN I think I might be.

ALICE You heard the girl. She's tired. It's all this school work. You can't have a social life and study for 'A' levels. I know that. You shouldn't go dragging her out on a night like this. You take up too much of her time. Chris. She's got enough on with her schoolwork.

HELEN I might have an early night.

ALICE You do. Looks as if you've got your marching orders, young man.

She gives **Chris** *his coat.*

Chris *throws up his hands in mock defeat and backs out.* **Helen** *follows him as if to front door.*

HELEN I'm sorry about Mum. Don't take it personally.

CHRIS It's not your mum I'm worrying about. Come here, Nell. *He puts his arms round her* What's wrong?

HELEN Nothing. Nothing, honestly.

CHRIS You've been so strange. I feel terrible. I thought you were going off me. You'd tell me, wouldn't you, if you were going off me? If there was somebody else?

HELEN There's nobody else. Don't be daft.

CHRIS Then what is it?

HELEN I can't tell you.

ALICE *off* Helen!

HELEN I'll see you Wednesday. After school.

Chris *backs away. From a distance, they both stand frozen watching each other. Music. Then at the same time they both turn away, each hurt and puzzled, and go off.*

School playground noise, etc. **Ruthlyn** *comes on, looking round.* **Chris** *enters with schoolbag, from the other side, also looking round.*

CHRIS Ruthlyn! Have you seen Helen?

RUTHLYN She went a bit funny in afternoon registration and Miss Clancy sent her home. She asked me to let you know.

CHRIS What d'you mean, funny?

RUTHLYN   Just funny. Just a bit funny. She asked me to give you her love and she'll see you soon.

CHRIS   I'll go round there now.

RUTHLYN   I wouldn't. Leave her a bit.

CHRIS   I'll phone her then.

RUTHLYN   Wait for her to phone you, she said.

CHRIS   Ruthlyn. What's happening?

RUTHLYN   *sorry for him*   I don't know, Chris, and that's the truth. I don't know.

She goes.

***Chris** goes off in opposite direction.*

***Helen** is lit in her room writing a letter. She speaks to the audience at first, becoming more and more withdrawn.*

HELEN   February 27th
Dear . . .
She pauses, thinking
. . . Nobody,
At home there's a tap in the bathroom that won't switch off properly. Sometimes you don't hear it at all, and sometimes it keeps you awake all night, drip, drip, drip, regular and slow and insistent. And that's how I feel about you. It's like footsteps in the dark. I don't know whether you're there at all. But the thought that you might be there is a drip, drip, drip that won't go away, day and night, day and night, a clock that never stops ticking. Pregnant, pregnant, what if I'm pregnant, tick tock tick tock tick . . .
I'm so frightened at night that I can hardly breathe. I can't tell anyone.
You're only a shadow. You're only a whisper. Leave me alone. I don't want you.
Go away. Please, please, go away.

*She goes to stage centre and **Chris** joins her. They hold hands.*

CHRIS   Are you sure?

HELEN   No. Of course I'm not sure. I don't know about anything.

CHRIS   It'll be all right, I'll stay with you, whatever happens.

HELEN   I was horrible to you. I'm sorry. I was frightened. I didn't know what to say to you.

CHRIS   I was frightened too. I thought you wanted to finish with me.

HELEN   Oh Chris!

CHRIS   You're probably mistaken about it. It might be just worry. It's too soon to know, isn't it?

HELEN   I don't know. I just don't know.

CHRIS   I wish I'd been more careful . . .

HELEN   Not just you. It was my fault, too.

CHRIS   We were so stupid! It's not as if we're a pair of kids. But you'll be all right. I know you will.

He kisses her and leaves her, and she stands centre stage. We are aware that she is lonely and afraid. She goes.

Music denotes another day.

Helen and **Ruthlyn** *enter from opposite sides.*

RUTHLYN   Hi stranger!

HELEN   Oh Ruthlyn! Hi.

RUTHLYN   You feeling better?

HELEN   Yes, thanks. Fine.

RUTHLYN   You look awful.

HELEN   Thanks.

RUTHLYN   Chris looks awful too.

HELEN   Does he?

RUTHLYN   Not had a row with him, have you?

HELEN   No, course I haven't.
  Ruthlyn . . . I . . .

RUTHLYN   What?

HELEN   Oh, it's nothing. I'm just worrying about my exams.

RUTHLYN   Your exams! Helen! You've no need to worry about them! You're brilliant, you are! Hey, we're going to be late.

HELEN   I'm not coming to school, Ruthlyn . . . I've got to do something.

RUTHLYN   *shrugs*   See you then.

Leaves her.

Helen *makes up her mind and goes into a chemist's shop. She is picking up and reading packets, putting them down again. She is approached by a **male shop assistant**.*

ASSISTANT   Can I help you?

HELEN   Oh . . . No thanks. I'm just looking.

ASSISTANT   Did you want one of those?

HELEN   No. I . . . er . . . I'd like some throat sweets please.

ASSISTANT   Then you're looking on the wrong counter.

HELEN   Am I?

ASSISTANT   Well, these are home pregnancy tests. They won't do your throat much good.

HELEN   No. I don't suppose they will.

ASSISTANT   Are you feeling all right?

HELEN   Yes. No. Actually, I will take one of these. I think my friend wants one.

Assistant leaves. *Helen* leaves shop area.

Helen tries to read the packet surreptitiously, then guiltily stuffs it into her pocket. *Alice* approaches. She is wearing outdoor clothes.

ALICE   Helen? Where've you been?

HELEN   Shops. That's all.

ALICE   Chris has phoned twice. He seems to think you're not well.

HELEN   I'm all right.

ALICE   You don't look all right. You look terrible.

HELEN   I told you, Mum. I'm all right. I wish everyone would leave me alone!

ALICE   *shocked at **Helen's** outburst*   I'll see you after work.

She goes.

Helen, alone, goes to her bed. She takes out her package, reading the instructions, preparing the test tube etc.

HELEN   March 22nd
Dear Nobody,
Somehow I managed to read the instructions and hold things the right way up and do it. Then I had to wait five minutes. *She sets an alarm clock.*   Have you any idea how long five minutes last? The silence in my house while I sat looking at my watch was like that deathly quiet you get in a three-hour exam. Three hours when you read and read the questions and you don't know any of the answers. I tried to think of all the things people would be doing

during that time.

Mum would be typing away on her computer keyboard at the bank. Dad would be filing books away at the library, humming a jazz tune to himself. Grandad would be making himself a cup of tea, stirring and stirring the leaves in his teapot the way he does, peering down into its steam. Ruthlyn would be in maths, where I should be. And Chris. What were *you* doing Chris, while my test tube was concocting its brew?

Alarm goes.

All leave stage.

Tom *runs on in climbing gear.* **Chris** *joins him.*

TOM Hi, Chris! Good man. You're coming climbing then?

CHRIS No. I've never done any. I thought I'd just watch.

TOM You'll learn, dope-head. Don't tell me you're scared.

CHRIS Course I'm not scared. My mother's a climber, you know. She's very well known.

Chris *watches as* **Tom** *begins to climb.*

TOM Come on, Chris! It's easy.

Chris *makes a poor attempt and slides off. They both joke about it. Then, as* **Tom** *continues to climb,* **Chris** *crouches down, takes a pen and paper out of his small rucksack and begins to write.*

Joan *appears at side of stage and reads letter to* **Don**.

JOAN Dear Joan,
I'm just having a breather after a session at the climbing wall. I twisted my ankle a bit because I came down a bit fast, but when it's better I think I'll get to the top easily. I think climbing must be in my blood. Did you climb in Derbyshire when you lived down here? I expect you climb in the Lake District now.

Tom joins **Chris**.

TOM Too much for you?

CHRIS Great. It was a synch.

TOM You came off it pretty quick.

CHRIS I remembered I had a letter to write to my mother.

TOM Excuses!

CHRIS We often write to each other.

TOM Fancy a drink?

CHRIS I've got a *Hamlet* essay to do.

TOM Haven't we all? Come on, you need a pint. Drown your sorrows, whatever they are . . . Come on, Chris. What's up?

CHRIS Nothing's up.

TOM I'm going cycling in France this summer. Don't fancy coming, do you?

CHRIS Nope.

TOM We always said we'd do it after the 'A's. You're fit enough, aren't you? You were dead keen before the mocks.

CHRIS I've gone off it, that's all.

TOM What's on your mind?

CHRIS I was just thinking. What if Hamlet had got Ophelia pregnant?

TOM Good grief! Good grief, Chris!

They go.

JOAN *continues reading letter* Maybe I'll come up and see you when I'm more experienced and you can show me the ropes! Joking apart, I would like to pop in and see you some time. *Joan registers a little anxiety. She had been both wanting and dreading this.* Your son, Christopher.

*She and **Don** go.*

***Alan** enters.*

HELEN Mr Marshall. Hi! Is Chris in?

ALAN Hello there, love. I didn't hear you. No, he's out at the moment. Playing on a climbing frame or something.

HELEN Oh. *She is obviously disappointed.*

ALAN Do you want to leave him a message?

HELEN Could you tell him it's all right. Tell him everything's fine.

ALAN Will do. Sit and wait for a bit though, he shouldn't be long.

Swirly, fainty music.

***Alan** has his back to her.*

HELEN *weak* It's hot in here, could I have a drink? Mr Marshall. It's hot in here, could I have a drink?

She tries to push her way out as if something is surrounding her. She faints.

ALAN Helen!

***Alan** helps her off. She goes to her bed.*

*Chris enters as **Alan** returns to his wheel.*

CHRIS Hi Dad! I'm home!

ALAN Your Helen was here just now. I've just taken her back home. She fainted.

CHRIS Fainted! Is she all right?

ALAN She is now. She was as white as a sheet, poor kid.

CHRIS I'll go round there.

ALAN Do no such thing. An early night is all she needs. Probably too much studying. She left you a message, anyway. 'Tell Chris everything's all right,' she says.

*He goes, leaving **Chris** standing centre stage as music blasts on. **Chris** raises his fists in triumph.*

CHRIS Helen! It's all right! Everything's all right!

HELEN *in her room* You don't exist. You're nobody. So why? Why?

HELEN *writing* March 30th
Dear Nobody,
After school today I went to town on my own and bought another pregnancy test.

*Chris leaves stage and **Alice** enters, as if working in the kitchen, humming to herself.*

HELEN I lifted out the stick, but I knew before I looked at it what colour it would be.

Slowly Helen goes to join Alice and stands watching her.

Pink. Positive. Yesterday negative. Today positive. She ought to know. Of all people, Mum ought to know.

ALICE There you are. I thought you were out.

HELEN Mum. I want to tell you something.

ALICE Chris rang up about half an hour ago. He said if you come in he wants to meet you in the park at five.

HELEN Something's happened, Mum.

ALICE Off you go, young lady. I thought you and Chris had had a row, the way you've been behaving. Go and make it up with him.

HELEN Mum . . .

ALICE *laughing, impatient* Off you go, Helen.

HELEN *tries to put her arms round her mother, very upset* I wish you'd let me tell you . . .

ALICE *not at all demonstrative, a little shocked at this display* What's all this about?

HELEN Mum . . .

ALICE Off you go. I've got a meal to cook. Don't keep the young man waiting.

Alice goes.

Helen stands, distraught.

Chris comes to her, put his arms round her.

CHRIS Don't talk. Let me just hold you. I've missed you. It's been days and days.

HELEN I did a test, and it was negative. Then I fainted at your dad's. I did another test and it was positive. How can something be negative and positive? I don't understand.

CHRIS Neither do I.

HELEN Chris. It means I'm pregnant.

CHRIS I love you.

*They stand apart, watching each other. As **Helen** turns away he knows that she feels more alone than ever.*

HELEN *standing with her back to **Chris**, speaking to audience* It was as if he couldn't think of anything else to say.

CHRIS *to audience* What else could I say to her? A baby is. A baby's not. Something and nothing. Somebody and nobody. Now and forever. Life began three thousand six hundred million years ago. Life began in January. And I'm the father. I tried to wake myself up to the sound of that word, and I couldn't. It was meaningless. It meant I was responsible.

HELEN *afraid and determined* April 1st
Dear Nobody,
Last night I decided what I must do.

CHRIS It meant Newcastle slipping away from me like a vanishing dream. I felt like a mouse crouching into a tiny hole. I felt the mousy air suffocating me. We'll be all right. Whatever happens. I won't leave you. Helen, oh Helen, what have we done?

He goes.

HELEN I don't ask your forgiveness for this. I'm going to get rid of you.

*The next scene represents a horse-ride in which **Helen** is eventually thrown.*

*Ruthlyn enters but stands at side watching **Helen**.*

HELEN   I went riding with Ruthlyn. She didn't know what I had in my mind.

Other actors may create the galloping sound by drumming their hands on desks or boxes. It must be threatening.

HELEN   Come on Nab! Come on Nab! Faster, faster, faster!

Galloping sound increases.

RUTHLYN   *shouting*   Rein him in! Rein him in!

HELEN   *shouting*   Go away from me, Nobody! Go away! Leave me alone!

RUTHLYN   *shouting*   Helen! Rein him in!

HELEN   *panicking*   I can't! I can't stop it!   *She screams.*

Sudden silence.

*Ruthlyn runs to **Helen** and helps her to sit down. **Helen** is comforted by her.*

*All leave except for **Helen** and **Ruthlyn***

RUTHLYN   Are you all right? You look terrible.

HELEN   *clutching her stomach*   Yes, I'm all right.

RUTHLYN   Well you don't look all right. Do you want to lie down or something?

Helen is obviously not listening to her but stands with her arms wrapped round herself.

RUTHLYN   You can tell me, you know. You can trust me.

Helen shakes her head, goes slowly over to her bed and sits down, still doubled over.

RUTHLYN   Shall I get your mum?

HELEN   No. Don't get her.

RUTHLYN   You've got to talk to somebody, Helen. You ought to talk to your mum, you know. I tell my mum everything. Just look for the right moment, and tell her. Whatever it is.

Ruthlyn goes.

Helen sits on her bed, inert.

*Alice enters her kitchen and prepares food. **Helen** takes up her flute or other instrument and begins to play, sadly.*

ALICE   *off*   Helen! Tea!

HELEN   I don't want any. I'm not hungry.

*Alice comes into **Helen's** room. Stands with her arms folded,* *looking down at **Helen**.*

ALICE Why aren't you hungry?

HELEN I don't know. I just don't want anything.

ALICE You didn't want anything last night.

HELEN I'm all right.

ALICE You were sick this morning.

HELEN Mum, I told you . . .

ALICE I want to know what's going on.

HELEN I'm starting a new project. Miss Clancy said I could start the background work at home.

ALICE I don't give a damn about Miss Clancy. What's going on, Helen?

HELEN Can't you guess?

ALICE I can guess. I'd like to have heard it from you, but I can guess. How many times have you done it?

HELEN Does it matter?

ALICE Yes, it does matter, for goodness sake! It matters to me! And you've never heard of decency? Did you have to do it? After all I've taught you?

HELEN *matching her mother's anger* We didn't think. It just happened.

***Helen** is biting her nails. **Alice** slaps her. She turns away from **Helen**, overcome with emotion and too upset to speak.*

HELEN Mum . . . I'm sorry. It's not your fault. None of this is your fault.

ALICE What are we going to do with you, child?

*The emotion of that moment is broken by the sound of **Ted Garton** playing jazz piano. He calls as he plays.*

TED Helen! Where's Helen? Some new music for you! I picked it up at the library today!

***Alice** and **Helen** walk past **Ted** with their coats on, **Helen** much subdued.*

TED There you are. You'll love this! You're not going out, are you?

ALICE She is. And she's in no mood to be playing that sort of music, I can tell you.

*Puzzled, still playing, **Ted** watches them go.*

Doctor's surgery.

***Helen** takes off her coat and shoes. Her mother sits watching.*

Helen goes behind a screen.

Ted opens the door to Chris.

TED   Hello there Chris! How's the guitar coming on?

CHRIS   Not bad, Mr Garton. Is Helen in?

TED   Ready to join my jazz band yet, are you?

CHRIS   Can't do jazz chords. They're too hard. Is she in?

TED   Helen? No, she's gone out with her mother. Bursting with secrets, the pair of them.

CHRIS   Is she all right?

TED   Course she's all right! Come on in a minute, and I'll go through some chords with you. We don't see enough of you, these days. Nice chords these. Just listen. Beautiful chords.

Doctor emerges from behind screen.

DOCTOR   You can get dressed now, Helen.

HELEN   Thank you, doctor.

DOCTOR   She's probably twelve weeks pregnant, Mrs Garton.

HELEN   *weak after the anger and emotion of the last scene* I don't want a baby. I don't want a baby.

DOCTOR   If a termination is to take place it must be before sixteen weeks. Otherwise it will be very traumatic for you.

Very much apart, and both distressed, Helen and Alice stand up to leave the surgery.

TED   Come on Chris. You're not concentrating. Music's the only thing that matters, you know. Once you've understood that, you've understood everything. Helen understands it. Nothing will come between her and her music.

Chris and Ted are playing guitar, Chris very badly, as Helen and Alice walk in. Chris jumps up, pleased.

TED   There. I told you she wouldn't be long. Play her your new tune!

ALICE   Upstairs, young lady.

Helen looks helplessly at Chris, brushes past him and goes to her room, where she lies on her bed.

TED   What's up?

ALICE   Never you mind, what's up. And as for you, young man, I want you out of this house this minute.

CHRIS Can I have a word with Helen, Mrs Garton?

ALICE No. She has nothing to say to you, and you have nothing to say to her.

Ted, embarrassed, hums his way out of the room, looks in the direction of Helen's room, and decides not to interfere. He goes.

ALICE I want you to know that you're never to come to this house again. She's decided to have an operation. Do you understand?

CHRIS You must let me speak to her, Mrs Garton. I must talk to her.

ALICE No, Chris. Go on. Go home. You're not welcome here.

They stare at each other. At last Chris turns away. As he gets to his room and chair he begins to compose a letter.

CHRIS Darling, darling Helen.

Alice goes into Helen's room, speaking to her as if she was a small child.

ALICE No one will know. Daddy won't know. I've arranged everything. It will all be over by the end of the week.

CHRIS *writing* It's my baby too. It's a little egg. It's life itself.

ALICE *to Helen* You want to get it all over with quickly, don't you? You're not going to make a fuss, are you?

CHRIS *writing* Two hundred million sperm tried to reach you, and this is the one that made it. Nothing will ever be exactly like it again, ever, ever, in the world. It is unique.

ALICE Think of your future. It's your future. You mustn't throw it away. *She goes.*

HELEN *to herself* My future is a deep, black well. Whatever I see in it frightens me.

CHRIS *writing* It is me in you, Helen, and you in me. I love you, whatever you do. *Finishes writing.*

CHRIS *narration* I couldn't read it afterwards. I felt blitzed, as if I'd been listening to crashing music and all of a sudden there was so much silence that I could drown in it.

Alice brings a bag into Helen's room and puts into it a nightdress, slippers and wash bag. Helen doesn't move.

At same time:

Chris is climbing. Great sense of fear and also recklessness. At one point he stretches out as if hanging by one arm.

Alice holds out Helen's coat for her. As if in a dream Helen puts it on.

CHRIS   The stars were out, kind of shivering. The moon was like a white face with a crooked smile, and I'm not kidding, those stars were like rocks. They were massive that night, white hanging rocks that could come crashing down from the sky at any minute.

At that point Helen and her mother come out of the house. They are both wearing coats, and Alice is carrying the suitcase.

HELEN   Dear Nobody,
You did not ask for this. I have nothing to give you. Nothing. With all my heart I'm sorry.

ALICE   It will all be over soon. Then you can get on with your life again.

CHRIS   *shouting*   Bastard! Bastard! Bastard!   *Echo*

ACT TWO

Helen is standing by her bed in her nightdress.

HELEN   April 10th
Dear Nobody,
It feels as if this is the last day of my life. All the way here
Mum never stopped talking. It was as if she was
frightened of silence. And all the time she was jabbering, I
was forcing this into my head: this is simply an operation
to remove unwanted cells from my body. That's all it is.
When I parked the car in the grounds of the hospital there
was a dead bird on the grass verge, a tiny skinny thing
without feathers.

Alice and the Nurse come into the room as she is speaking.

NURSE   Good girl, you have your nightie on. Pop into bed
now. I think we have all her details, Mrs Garton.

ALICE   And I'll take your clothes, Helen.

NURSE   She can put them in her locker, Mrs Garton,
there's no need . . .

ALICE   I'll take them.

HELEN   Mum . . . Stay with me.

She is scared, would like her mother to embrace her.

ALICE   Now don't make a fuss, Helen. It'll be over in no
time.

*Alice is moved but kisses Helen briefly and leaves with the
Nurse.*

HELEN   You are twelve weeks old. You are like a little
pink tadpole. You will be about nine centimetres long. You
weigh about fourteen grammes.
Oh Nobody, when I think of the day when I went riding on
Nab – I'm ashamed. Why didn't you go then? Why didn't
you go away?
You didn't think about anything and you didn't know
anything and you clung on. I feel as if you knew something
that I will never understand. I've become two people. I'm
so lonely, Nobody. I'm so frightened.

Lights darken and change.

Nurse enters with trolley and syringe.

NURSE   Just move your arm a moment, dear. That's it.

HELEN   What's it for?

NURSE   You're going to have your operation now. It'll all be over soon.

HELEN   *panicking*   I want Chris.

NURSE   Hold yourself still dear. It won't take a minute.

HELEN   Please let me talk to Chris.

NURSE   It won't hurt. It'll all be over soon and you can go home with your mam.

HELEN   It's not too late, is it? Please let me talk to him. Please don't let it be too late.

NURSE   I think I'd better fetch someone.   *Goes.*

*Helen gets out of bed and goes straight to the locker, roots round for her clothes, realises her mother has taken them, and runs from the room. The **Nurse** comes in with a **Doctor**. They look round hurriedly, then run out.*

Later that day.

*Music. **Helen**, dressed properly, enters, ecstatic.*

HELEN   We're free! We're free! Little Nobody, I'll never let you go now!

*Park. **Chris** walks on, head down, bag slung over shoulder.*

HELEN   Chris.

For a moment they just look at each other. He is still hurt and accusing, shocked to see her.

HELEN   Chris. It's all right.

He doesn't understand.

HELEN   I'm going to keep it! I ran out of the hospital – in my nightie!

They both laugh. They come together and embrace.

HELEN   I didn't know what to do. I just let Mum take over.

CHRIS   I couldn't even talk to you. She took you away from me. She hates me for what I've done to you.

HELEN   She'll hate me for what I've done to her, Chris. I didn't want to hurt her. But somebody had to be hurt.

CHRIS   What do we do now?

HELEN   I don't know. You think of something.

CHRIS   We could always go and live in that cave out on the moors.

HELEN   That's just your trouble, Chris. You're too romantic. We've got to be practical about this.

CHRIS   I've only got twenty pounds. And a birthday coming up in August. I'll get a summer job.

HELEN   There's nothing going round here, and you know it. Most of the people in your street haven't got jobs at all, at any time of the year, let alone in the summer.

CHRIS   I'll go down south. I'll get something.

HELEN   And after that? When the baby's come? What do we do then? We'll be parents, Chris!

They are both suddenly aware of the enormity of the situation.

*As they turn away from each other, both fathers come onto stage. **Alan** sits at one side, looking through photographs. **Ted** is playing the piano. Both **Helen** and **Chris** go up to their fathers and stand, hesitating, in front of them.*

CHRIS   When I got home that night Dad was looking through a box of old photographs. I felt I was half drowning. His voice was like a piece of driftwood keeping me afloat.

ALAN   Come and have a look at these, Chris. They'll make you laugh, some of them.

TED   Helen. Why aren't you with your mother?

HELEN   Dad, I haven't been to Auntie Pat's. I've been to hospital.

TED   Hospital! But your mother didn't say anything . . .

HELEN   It was an abortion clinic. I walked out.

TED   I don't understand.

HELEN   Dad. I'm going to have a baby.

TED   Helen!

***Ted** stops playing. Overwhelmed and disbelieving, he goes towards her. She can no longer face him.*

ALAN   I looked like you when I was your age, Chris. Just look at this one.

CHRIS   I didn't want to look at anything. I didn't even want to open my eyes. I knew which photograph Dad was talking about even without looking.

ALAN   My dad took this! Me in my army uniform! Look at me, short haircut, proud excited smile, off to do National Service.

CHRIS   He did look like me. I used to look at it and think of him as a man. He wasn't. He was a boy with a fresh face and a shy smile.

Helen goes to the piano and starts playing. Alice comes in, glances at Helen and then walks past her, not looking at her, and off.

TED   Your mother's very upset, Helen.

HELEN   Of course she's upset. But will she let me stay here?

TED   Good God, she's not going to kick you out into the streets.

HELEN   But will she let me live here, with my baby?

TED   You're not really going to keep it, love?

CHRIS   *absently*   Was it in the war, Dad?

ALAN   Was it heck! I'm not that old. Don't know myself. It feels like another lifetime. Thought the whole world was mine, in those days. Just like you do. Chris.

CHRIS   Dad . . .

ALAN   Only your chances are better than mine ever were. Make the most of them. You can never start again.

Chris wants to tell him, but recognises that the moment is not right. Helpless, he turns away.

Helen is playing the piano. Ted shouts over her playing, though he is not used to raising his voice.

TED   I'd have given anything in the world to go to music school. Do you know that? You're throwing your life away.

Helen and Chris each go to their rooms.

Ted and Alan leave the stage.

Helen sits on her bed, distressed. Chris sits in his chair.

Alice brings Ted his coat and marches him to Alan's door. He opens it.

ALICE   I expect you're Chris's father.

ALAN   That's right, I am.

ALICE   I'm Helen's mother. This is her father.

ALAN   Oh, how do you do? Pleased to meet you both.

ALICE   *ignoring his proffered hand*   There's something we need to get straight.

ALAN   *surprised*   You'd better come in.

All three go off stage

CHRIS *writing* Dear Joan,
Forgive me for writing to you again but there is something I really need to tell you.

He rips up the letter.

CHRIS Why aren't you here! You should be here!

Ruthlyn enters.

RUTHLYN Hey, Chris! There's a gig on at the Leadmill tonight. Fancy coming?

CHRIS No. I need some kip.

RUTHLYN You're turning into an old man. It'll be life insurance and a mortgage next.

CHRIS Look, I don't feel like it, right?

RUTHLYN That's just what Helen said. Have you two split or something?

CHRIS Don't be daft. Course we haven't.

RUTHLYN You used to be good fun, you two. Come and enjoy yourself, Chris. You'll be dead before you know it.

She goes. Chris gazes after her ruefully. Sounds of gig in distance. He's very torn. He goes off.

Gig. Afro-Caribbean music. Tom and Ruthlyn are dancing and laughing. Helen and Chris come on, hand in hand. Delighted, Tom and Ruthlyn draw them in to dance. Taking up the whole area, they eventually dance off.

Chris's house. Alan comes on, very depressed. He sits down in a chair, weary to the bone.

Chris comes home, whistling. He opens the door.

ALAN Chris? Here a minute.

CHRIS What's up, Dad?

ALAN I wish you'd told me. That woman comes here, shouting her mouth off. Says you've got to marry Helen. I don't know what the hell's going on, do I?

CHRIS *lost for words* I wanted to tell you.

ALAN You wanted to tell me! The thing about lads is that they can get away scot free if they want to. Or they think they can.

CHRIS I don't want to.

ALAN So what are you planning to do about it? Are you telling me you want to get wed, at the age of eighteen? What do you want then? What about your degree? What about Newcastle? You're not expecting to take her with

35

you, are you? Away from her family and her pals? What would she do, that lass, stuck in a student's bedsit in the middle of Newcastle. Stuck in with a baby? She's reckoned to be a very clever lass, that Helen.

CHRIS She is. She's brilliant.

ALAN Are you expecting her to throw up all her chances too? What the hell were you thinking of?

Chris, his back to his father, breaks down.

ALAN Her mother says either you marry the girl or you're not to see her again. I can't say I blame her. Mind you, what's done is done.

He comes over to Chris, puts both his hands on Chris's shoulders, briefly gentle, but too distressed and angry to hug him properly.

ALAN Don't think I'm not sorry for you.

He and Chris both leave the stage.

Alice and Helen come on from opposite sides. Helen is looking at herself full-length in a mirror. She can't fasten her skirt. When she sees Alice's reflection she laughs self-consciously.

HELEN Hi Mum. It's a bit tight, this!

Alice immediately turns away and goes off.

HELEN May 15th
Dear Nobody,
I've lost my mum. We walk past each other like strangers in the house. We don't talk, because she doesn't want to hear about you. And because we don't talk about you, we don't talk about anything. It's my fault, all this. I wish I could tell her I'm sorry.

Sounds of train station.

She joins Chris. They sit down opposite each other, as if they are on a train.

CHRIS I didn't really think you'd come, you know.

HELEN Of course I came!

HELEN How do you feel, Chris? Are you nervous?

CHRIS As hell.

HELEN It'll be all right.

CHRIS How about you? How d'you feel?

HELEN I'm OK. I'm fine.

CHRIS   You look OK. You look great.

Helen laughs, not believing him, but pleased.

CHRIS   It's great to see you smiling again, Nell.

They sit holding hands. They lean back, contented to be with each other.

Joan and Don come on side of stage. Joan is obviously nervous. Don comes to her and holds her hand.

JOAN   They'll be here soon.

DON   Are you nervous?

JOAN   I am, Don. Very.

DON   You'll be all right. You're doing the right thing.

CHRIS   This is our stop, Helen.

Chris and Helen stand up and move across the stage.

JOAN   They're here.

She is nervous.

JOAN   Christopher!

CHRIS   Hello . . . Joan. This is Helen.

JOAN   It's so good to see you at last. Don! Here he is! My son, Christopher.

DON   How do you do, Christopher. Pleased to meet you.

CHRIS   This is Helen.

JOAN   Hello Helen. I'm very pleased you could come, both of you. Well! Where do we start!

DON   With a cup of coffee, I should think.

HELEN   No thanks. Not for me. I don't like coffee at the moment.

JOAN   Tea, then. That's all right. We can make both. It's not good for you, too much coffee.

HELEN   I don't drink it at the moment because it tastes strange.

CHRIS   Not yet, Helen.

HELEN   I'm pregnant, you see.

DON   Good God!

The scene changes as they enter the house. Helen sits in another room. Don coasts.

Joan and Chris, a little embarrassed, try to get to know each other again.

JOAN   Well. I'm lost for words. I didn't expect this!

They both laugh, embarrassed.

CHRIS I suppose it was a bit of a shock.

JOAN How are things at home? Your dad?

CHRIS He's fine. Fine. Dad's fine. Is Helen all right?

DON She just wanted a bit of fresh air. I'll pop out and have a chat with her in a minute.

He goes.

JOAN I admire you for coming, Chris. It was brave of you. You're braver than me.

CHRIS I've been wanting to see you for ages. Before, you know, before Helen was . . . you know.

JOAN I think of you as a little boy of ten with a passion for model trains and Batman, with a little high voice and a freckly face, and I meet a young man who is in love and who is about to father a child. What will you do?

CHRIS I don't know.

JOAN What do you want to do?

CHRIS Everything. I want to do my degree at Newcastle. And I want to be with Helen. I don't really know what she wants. She doesn't know.

JOAN Does Alan know about this?

CHRIS Yes, he does. He . . . I . . . I let him down. That's how he feels.

JOAN He'll be upset. He's a very traditional man, your father. A bit old-fashioned.

CHRIS *defensively* He was great about it, though.

JOAN I'm sure he was.

The atmosphere is very tense.

JOAN Christopher. I know you think I did a terrible thing when I left your father.

Chris *doesn't know what to say.*

JOAN But before that I had done an even worse thing, and that was to marry him in the first place. *pause* Can I tell you about it?

CHRIS If you want to.

JOAN I was probably younger than Helen when I met Alan. My dad died when I was twelve. My mum couldn't cope after that. I left school at sixteen. I met your father at work. He was one of the workers and I was an office girl. He used to come and sit by me in the yard at lunchtime and talk to me. Do you know, I think he reminded me of my dad? He was ten years older than me, and very quiet and sensitive. He thought the world of me; he adored me. And I thought I loved him. Maybe I did, but it wasn't the right kind of love.

CHRIS *bitterly* And then you met Don.

JOAN I met Don.

CHRIS You didn't want to see me again.

JOAN I couldn't see you, not when you were little. I felt terrible about leaving Alan. I couldn't take his son away from him as well. How could I have done that to him?

Don enters.

CHRIS I think I ought to go. I'll get Helen.

JOAN No, don't go yet. Why don't you stay here and have a chat with Don? I'll go and sit with Helen for a bit.

She goes.

*Don sits by **Chris**. They nod at one another then sit in awkward silence.*

DON Sheffield's doing well, I see.

CHRIS Is it?

DON Two teams heading for the cup-final.

CHRIS Ah. Yes.

DON *laughs* Come on Chris. Come and give me a hand with the washing-up.

They go.

*Joan enters the area where **Helen** is sitting.*

JOAN Hello, Helen.

HELEN Oh, hello.

JOAN Do you mind if I join you?

HELEN No, it's fine. It's lovely out here. Peaceful. I didn't think you'd be able to see mountains from your house.

JOAN Oh. yes. I couldn't live far away from mountains. Christopher tells me you're in the sixth form too, Helen.

HELEN I was.

JOAN And your exams start next month?

HELEN I won't be taking them.

JOAN Why not? You look well enough to me.

HELEN How can I? What's the point?

JOAN Helen, there's every point. What's the point of

giving it all up? Take your chance. You owe it to yourself, and to your mum and dad. And you owe it to this little person in here. *She pats **Helen's** stomach.* I hope you do well, Helen.

*__Joan__ goes. **Helen** stares after her. She is surprised and elated.*

HELEN Did you feel that, Nobody? Did you hear it? That was your grandmother talking! I owe it to myself. I owe it to you, she says!

*__Chris__ comes to join **Helen**.*

They are on the train again.

HELEN Chris and I were very quiet, going home on the train. I think he thought I was asleep. But I wasn't. I was planning my revision timetable. I've already got my full offer at the music college. I could still go there. We'll do it together, little Nobody. We'll do it!

CHRIS Helen was asleep on the way back. I was glad. I didn't want to talk. My head was full of all kinds of things. But first, first, I had to get the exams over.

*__Helen__ and **Chris** separate. **Tom** joins **Chris**. They are about to go into the exam room.*

TOM All set, Chris? Ready for battle?

CHRIS No way. Haven't done a stroke.

TOM Who's the old guy who gets stabbed?

CHRIS Get lost, Tom.

TOM Is *Hamlet* the play with the balcony scene?

CHRIS You're making me as nervous as hell.

TOM Good luck comrade.
'If it were done when 'tis done, then 'twere well
It were done quickly.'

*__Tom__ and **Chris** shake hands solemnly. They go to sit down.*

MR HARRINGTON *enters* Morning everyone. All fit for the big match? Right now . . . I'll just recite to you these rules and regs.

*__Helen__ comes on, looks round nervously, and is joined by **Ruthlyn**.*

*They are in a different room from **Chris** and **Tom**.*

RUTHLYN Good luck, Helen. I'm glad you decided to take them.

HELEN Am I mad, do you think? ‹

RUTHLYN   Course you're not mad! You'll sail through them, you will!

HELEN   It feels so weird to be back here. All the other girls are staring at me as if I've just walked in from outer space.

MR HARRINGTON   This is a three-hour examination.

HELEN   Dear Nobody,
Today two things happened to me. You moved. It was like a tiny bird fluttering. You are a little amazing piece of machinery.

MR HARRINGTON   Is there anyone who is not in a position to begin the examination?

Tom topples over.

MR HARRINGTON   Very funny, Tom. Perhaps you'd like me to wake you up when it's all over.

CHRIS   All of a sudden I felt calm. Helen was well and happy, after that terrible start. Did anything else matter?

HELEN   The other thing is this: I've decided that I must finish with Chris. I know I'm ready for you. I know I can cope. I was afraid of you once. Now, every inch of me wants you; you'll share my future with me. But I'm not ready for Chris. I'm not ready to share my life with him. I don't know what it is I'm more frightened of – promising myself to Chris forever, or spending forever without him.

MR HARRINGTON   Okay. Good luck, everyone. Do your best, eh. *Winking at Chris*   Now, the time is 9 am exactly . . .

HELEN   Six months ago the thought of spending the rest of our lives together had never entered our heads. We were a pair of kids having fun together. And now we've been catapulted into the world of grown-ups. I'm not ready for forever. When the exams are over, I'll tell him.

MR HARRINGTON   . . . and you may begin.

They all go, abruptly, as if the exam is finished.

Helen goes into the family living room.

TED   How did the exam go, Helen?

HELEN   Fine, it was fine.

ALICE   Fine! That's all you can ever say! Everything's fine for you!

TED   Alice, at least she's taking them. At least she hasn't given up.

ALICE   What good will they do her, that's what I want to know? What good is all that schooling now?

HELEN   I'm going out.

ALICE   Where to, young lady? You're not going to Chris's.

HELEN   I'm going to Nan's. Remember her? When did you last go to see her?

ALICE   It's none of your business. What happens between your nan and me is none of your business.

They go.

Nan *enters and sits in a chair.*

Helen *enters with* **Grandad**.

HELEN   I'm sorry I've not been round. I've been busy, you know, with my exams.

NAN   Why should you come here? Your mother never comes, from one year's end to the next. Why should you? And when's that baby of yours due?

GRANDAD   Dorrie? This is Helen you're talking to!

HELEN   I was going to tell you about it today, Nan.

NAN   There must be bad blood in our family. Like mother, like daughter.

HELEN   What d'you mean, Nan?

NAN   Ask your mother. I don't care. Not now.

They go.

Helen *goes to sit on her bed.*

Chris *and* **Tom** *enter. They are in the school yard.*

CHRIS   Thank God the exams are over.

TOM   Coming to the gig at the Leadmill tonight? Let's celebrate!

CHRIS   I don't know, Tom.

TOM   See if Helen and Ruthlyn can come. Have a laugh, for God's sake, after all that slog. Hell, you've got to come to France next month, dope-head.

CHRIS   Can't.

TOM   Why the hell not? I'll lend you the dosh if you're short.

CHRIS   It's not that.

TOM   What then? Helen? She'll not stop you. How're you going to manage when she's in Manchester and you're in Newcastle?

CHRIS She won't be going to Manchester this year, will she? And I wish to hell I wasn't going to Newcastle.

TOM Don't go then.

CHRIS What?

TOM If you feel that bad about it. Ask for a transfer to Sheffield. It's simple.

He leaves. **Chris** *stands, looking towards* **Helen's** *room. Music starts playing as* **Ruthlyn** *runs out and starts dancing. She is joined by* **Tom***.* **Helen** *enters, looks at* **Chris***, who holds out his hand to her.*

HELEN June 23rd
Dear Nobody,
I knew it had to be tonight. I tried to make it the best night we'd ever had together. I tried to let Chris know that he was the most special person in the world. I knew he was anxious. He knew something was up.

Zambian music. Dance.

CHRIS Helen, I've got something to tell you.

HELEN Later. Tell me later.

CHRIS I want to talk.

Ruthlyn *and* **Tom** *go.*

CHRIS Helen, I've got a plan for us. It was Tom's idea really, but it's brilliant. If you're staying in Sheffield next year, then I can too. We can be together all the time, Nell.

HELEN Chris. Chris, listen to me. I want us to finish.

The music stops.

HELEN I want us to finish.

They stare at each other, then **Helen** *turns away. She goes to her bed and stands by it.*

Chris *goes to his room.*

CHRIS *writing* Helen,
You have no right to do this to me. You can't shut me out of your life now. You can't pretend I don't exist. You can't keep me away. I won't stay away.

Darling Nell, I love you.

Helen, You can't mean it. Please don't mean it. Please see me again. Please let's talk.

Helen *lies on her bed, obviously weeping.*

CHRIS I wrote every day. She didn't answer. She hadn't

got the decency to answer. Suddenly I didn't exist.

TOM *comes to Chris* I'm sorry about you and Helen.

CHRIS I just feel so helpless. It's not as if I can do anything about it. She's made up her mind and that's that. I'm haunted by her. Every time I get on a bus I expect her to be on it. Every time I go into a room I think she's going to be there. I daren't go down the Moor, or to the Leadmill. It's as if she's been spirited away.

TOM She's a cow to do this to you.

CHRIS Stuff it, Tom.

TOM The offer's still on, you know. If you'd like to come to France, I'll lend you the dosh. Get away! It's the only thing you can do. Forget her.

They go, separately.

Helen is on her bed. The letters are spread out around her. Alice comes into the room with bedding. She sees Helen has been crying. She picks Chris's photograph up and puts it down again, face down as it was. As she goes to leave, Helen speaks to her.

HELEN Mum. I've finished with Chris.

ALICE I thought something like that had happened. I dare say you've done the right thing, for once. You're too young to be tied down, either of you. And you'd better set about arranging to have that baby adopted.

HELEN No. I won't do that.

ALICE Then what are you going to do?

HELEN I'm going to try for a University place in Sheffield. They have a crèche there. Maybe they'll even let me re-apply to Manchester to do Composition.

ALICE And what d'you think you're going to live on while all this is happening?

HELEN Grandad said I could have a room at his house if I wanted it.

ALICE That's no place for a baby. Nan sulking away in her bedroom the way she does. The place gives me the creeps.

HELEN Mum . . . When Nan found out I was having a baby she said 'like mother, like daughter'. She talked about bad blood in the family.

ALICE What are you trying to ask me, Helen?

HELEN Was I illegitimate?

ALICE As if I'd do a dirty thing like that.

44

HELEN   It isn't dirty.

ALICE   It is dirty. Stupid, sinful and dirty. If you must
know, Helen, I'm the one who was illegitimate, not you. I
was born out of wedlock, as they say. Born in sin. And I'll
never forgive my mother for that. I don't even know who
my father is.

HELEN   *shocked*   What do you mean? Grandad . . .?

ALICE   Your grandad married my mother when I was
about nine. And that, I can tell you, was a brave and
generous thing to do. In those days, an unmarried mother
was no more than a slut. Her child was a disgrace. My
mother's family wouldn't own her. She was an outcast, and
so was I. A bastard, that's what you were called if you
didn't have a father. That's what I was called, when I was
a child at school. That's the start I had in life. And that's
what you're doing to this baby you're having. We have no
choice about being born, remember. It's just something
that happens to us.

*She goes, followed by **Helen**.*

*Tom and **Chris** enter, on bicycles, wearing rucksacks.*

TOM   *singing*   Sur le pont d'Avignon
On y danse, on y danse . . .

*Tom stops and waits for **Chris** to catch him up.*

CHRIS   Stuff it, Tom. You sing like a crow, d'you know
that?

TOM   And you cycle like a frog, Marshall. Your knees are
supposed to be in the front of your legs, not the sides.
Didn't anyone ever tell you?

CHRIS   Corbeille!

TOM   Grenouille!

CHRIS   *singing*   Je te plumerai le bec . . .

TOM   *singing*   Je te plumerai les genoux . . .

BOTH   *cycle off, singing*   Allouete, gentille allouette . . .

They cycle back on and stop.

TOM   Campsite ahoy! Eh voila! Le camping!

*As they dismount and mime putting up tents **Helen** and
Ruthlyn come on. **Helen** lies on the floor and **Ruthlyn** holds
her ankles.*

RUTHLYN   I'm bored.

HELEN   I'm sorry Ruthlyn. The midwife says I've got to

practise my breathing exercises every day.

RUTHLYN *aping midwife* That's it, mothers. Relax, relax, relax. Breathe slowly. In out, in out, in. Fathers, watch how steadily they are breathing. Try to match your breathing to your wives'.

Hey, remember that baby on the bus! Wasn't it gorgeous! Can you believe it, in a couple of months you'll have one like that.

HELEN Its mother didn't have a ring on, did you notice? I wondered whether she was living on her own.

RUTHLYN Mind you, when it started that howling I could have cracked it one, I really could. It went right through me, all that screaming. Like a knife. You'd think she'd have been able to stop it. She just ignored it. Yours won't be like that. Eh? Your baby is going to be so cute!

She stands up, laughing.

Helen *turns away from her. It is as if she and* **Ruthlyn** *are miles apart.*

They go.

It is night-time. **Chris** *and* **Tom** *are lying in their tent.* **Tom** *is reading by the light of a torch.* **Chris** *is pretending to sleep.*

TOM Chris. Are you awake?

CHRIS No.

TOM Are you still missing her?

CHRIS Go to sleep.

TOM It's too hot to sleep. I've got a mouth full of baguette blisters and my bum's covered in saddle bruises. And I'm in love. How can I sleep?

CHRIS Oh, hell, Tom.

He switches on a torch and starts reading.

TOM You still reading that book of Mr Harrington's?

CHRIS Yeah. It's good. Brilliant..

TOM I don't see the point of reading about kids in the fifties! What's it got to do with us!

CHRIS I reckon all kids want to do that, don't they? Go burning off somewhere, anywhere. Just for the hell of it.

TOM *mocking* Finding themselves again at the other side. Passengers on the journey of life.

CHRIS Is there any point in making choices, do you think, or are we set on a track already?

TOM   Hell, it's too late to talk philosophy.

CHRIS   It's never too late.

TOM   Hey, dope, what d'you make of those Welsh girls in the next tent?

CHRIS   What Welsh girls?

TOM   Oh, Chris, you must have noticed!

CHRIS   Oh, the ones who keep talking Welsh. They're annoying the hell out of me.

TOM   I'm in love with Menai.

CHRIS   Love! It's about as much use as a flat tyre on a mountain bike. Go to sleep, Tom.

TOM   Yours isn't bad either. The little dark one. Bryn, her name is. Don't pretend you didn't see her. She couldn't take her eyes off you.

CHRIS   Oh, that one. She reminded me of Helen. I can't stop thinking about Helen. Does she give a damn what I'm doing?

Same night-time scene **Helen** *comes out with a dressing-gown on*

HELEN   July 17th

Dear Nobody,

I went out into the garden last night. The sky was clear, the stars looked enormous. Our garden was full of shadows, trees and moonlight and shadows, silver and velvet; lonely, quiet, humming shadows. I wanted to scream out into them. What will I do? I don't know where we're going to live, or what we're going to live on. I don't know how to look after you. I don't know if I'm strong enough for this. I'm frightened of the dark.

She stays.

Tom and Chris are outside the tent, another day. Bryn comes on, smiling, and Tom leaves, giving Chris a meaningful look. He carries on reading, pretending to ignore Bryn.

BRYN   What's that you're reading?

CHRIS   A book.

BRYN   I can see it's a book. I'm not stupid. Oh, *Catcher in the Rye*. I've read that.

CHRIS   So have I.

BRYN   What you reading it again for, then?

CHRIS   Because I'm bored with the company. Okay?

They freeze. Lights down on them.

HELEN *continuing her speech* I want Chris to hold me in his arms and say, it's all right, we'll manage, we can do it together. But I've turned my back on that, and nothing will stop day coming, nothing will stop you being born. You'll march into the world bursting with power and wisdom because you know how to be born. I don't know anything.

Bryn and Chris are a little shy of each other, sitting sunbathing by a river.

BRYN The world is made of gold, today. I don't want it to end, ever.

CHRIS I can't believe we've been here a week already.

BRYN Do you know something, Chris? I feel as if I've known you for ever.

CHRIS Where are Tom and Menai?

BRYN Oh, we lost them, miles back. Didn't you notice? Hey, Chris do you fancy a paddle in the river.

She takes off her shoes.

CHRIS Think I'll just watch.

BRYN *paddling* It's lovely! It's not a bit cold! Come on, Chris.

CHRIS But there are cows paddling in it down there!

BRYN *starting to splash Chris* If you don't come in willingly, you'll get wet anyway!

Bryn splashes and kicks water at Chris. He joins her in the water. They laugh. Freeze.

HELEN What's it like for you, Nobody, in the cool sea cave that's your home? Are you calm in there, and all crouched up safe? Are you rocked to sleep in the tide of my beating heart? You're a real person! I can't wait to see you!

Bryn and Chris laughing, climb out of the water and flop down onto the bank

BRYN Lie here. We'll soon dry off.

CHRIS It was good, that. You're good fun, Bryn.

BRYN You're good for me. I was really unhappy before, you know.

CHRIS Were you? Why was that?

BRYN My boyfriend and I packed up just before we came away. I never thought I'd be happy again . . . but, well . . . today's been fantastic.

CHRIS I know what you mean.

BRYN Have you got a girlfriend?

CHRIS Yes. Till last month.

BRYN What's she like?

CHRIS She's . . . brilliant.

BRYN Oh. Too clever for you then. Why did you finish?

CHRIS It was . . . it was . . . she just said she didn't want to see me again.

BRYN And are you very hurt about it?

CHRIS Yes. Very. I can't stop thinking about her.

BRYN Chris. *I* want you.

They embrace. **Bryn's** *kisses are passionate.* **Chris** *does not resist.*

Freeze.

HELEN August 8th
Dear Nobody,
It's too hot. I've turned into a tottering boat, a huge swaying galleon with round sails. Can I possibly get bigger than this and not burst? I saw a film once of a man stuffing himself with food till he exploded over all the people in the restaurant. I laughed at the time.

She and **Bryn** *both go.*

CHRIS Nell. I wanted you so much. And when I came back to Sheffield – where were you? You inhabited all the spaces of Sheffield, and yet you weren't there. Where were you?

Enter **Mr Harrington**, *the schoolteacher.*

MR HARRINGTON Hello there, Chris. French trip go well, did it?

CHRIS Yes, Mr Harrington. Brilliant. I've brought back the books you lent me, sir. Ace.

MR HARRINGTON Come back for your 'A' level results, have you? Seen 'em yet?

CHRIS No sir. Not yet. I was just going in . . .

MR HARRINGTON By God, I can't resist telling you! You got an A for English!

CHRIS An A! Brilliant! I can't believe it.

MR HARRINGTON I knew you could do it once you'd got used to Chaucer. Eh? Trust your old English master!

CHRIS It's all thanks to you, Mr Harrington.

MR HARRINGTON Not at all. Not at all. Mucked up your

Sociology though. Don't worry, you'll be all right.

CHRIS   A! I got an A!

MR HARRINGTON   So. What next? Newcastle, is it?

CHRIS   Yes, sir.

MR HARRINGTON   Make the most of it, won't you? It's all up to you now.

CHRIS   Yes, sir.

MR HARRINGTON   And where's your girlfriend off to? She's doing music, isn't she? Manchester?

CHRIS   She's having a baby, sir. We split.

MR HARRINGTON   Poor kid, Chris. Poor kid.

*He touches **Chris's** shoulder, sadly. Both go separately.*

***Helen** and **Nan** enter separately.*

NAN   I've got a present for you.

*She hands **Helen** a shawl.*

HELEN   Oh Nan! It's lovely! Was it yours, when you were a baby?

NAN   It was your mother's, but don't tell her I've kept it.

HELEN   Thank you.

NAN   Oh, you can't have it yet. How can I give it you before the baby's born? It might be dead!

She goes.

HELEN   Oh little thing, be alive! Be well. Be perfect for me.

***Joan** comes on stage with a letter.*

***Helen** sits down to play the piano, distractedly.*

***Alice** comes on, followed by **Ted**, who is carrying a baby cot. **Alice** is obviously displeased to see it. **Ted** struggles to set it up.*

ALICE   What's that cot doing here?

TED   It's for Helen's baby.

ALICE   Who says so?

TED   *slowly, straightening up and looking at her. I* say so.

HELEN   I'm staying here, then?

***Alice** turns away from her, disgusted.*

TED   *still looking at **Alice*** Of course she's staying here.

ALICE   Where else would you go, tell me that? This arrangement won't do for ever, just remember that. And don't leave that cot up. Not till it's born.

She goes.

TED   She has her own way of coping, Helen. Leave her.

HELEN   How can I stay here if I'm not wanted?

TED   Of course you're wanted. Get that out of your head. You're our daughter. Never forget that. It wasn't in our scheme of things to have a baby living in the house, but . . .

HELEN   It wasn't in my scheme of things either.

TED   We don't want to lose you, you know. You're to stay here as long as you want to. That's my promise. And your promise to me, Helen, is that you won't let your music go. Promise me that.

They embrace, and he goes.

Helen *plays, then freezes as lights come up on* ***Chris****, asleep.*

Bryn *enters and knocks.*

Alan *opens door.*

BRYN   Hi.

ALAN   *surprised*   Oh. Hello.

BRYN   I've come to see Chris. Is he in?

ALAN   Come in. Come in a minute. Chris? Wake up, sleeping beauty.

CHRIS   *waking up*   Mmm?

ALAN   There's someone to see you.

CHRIS   Tell him I'm dying.

ALAN   It's not a him.

He goes.

CHRIS   *to himself, dressing*   What? Tell her to hang on! It's Helen, it's Helen. Nell, oh Nell, I'm sorry.

Freeze as lights come up on ***Helen****.* ***Ruthlyn*** *runs to her.*

RUTHLYN   Helen! Three As! You're a genius, you are.

HELEN   Thanks Ruthlyn. I couldn't have done it if you hadn't lent me your notes. I'd missed so much.

RUTHLYN   How come I lend you my notes and I get Bs and you get As? Come on out for a bit, Helen. You can't hide away like this.

HELEN   I don't really feel like going out. I look so awful.

RUTHLYN   No you don't. You look fantastic! You're blooming! Come on, for a laugh.

*They freeze as **Chris** and **Bryn** come towards each other.*

BRYN Chris?

CHRIS *disappointed* Bryn!

BRYN Hi Slug! What time do you call this?

CHRIS What are you doing here?

ALAN Come to see you, it looks like.

He goes.

BRYN I'm on my way to Leeds, looking for accommodation for next year. When the train stopped at Sheffield I thought, hey! this is where Chris lives! So I just got off!

CHRIS I don't believe it.

BRYN Aren't you pleased to see me?

CHRIS Course I'm pleased to see you.

BRYN I wouldn't mind a cup of coffee.

CHRIS We could have one at Tom's. I was just going round there anyway.

*He puts a jacket on. They stand up. **Chris** is clearly unsure what to do.*

BRYN What's up?

CHRIS Nothing's up. It's the surprise, that's all. I didn't expect you.

BRYN Okay. So you don't like surprises. That's fair enough.

CHRIS I'm pleased you've come. Really I am.

BRYN You never answered my letters.

CHRIS I'm hopeless at letter writing.

Bryn holds out her hand then takes his impulsively.

Ruthlyn and Helen enter.

HELEN I'm sorry Ruthlyn. It's a bit hot for walking around.

RUTHLYN We'll go to Tom's if you like. He's always good for a laugh.

*Tom runs on, sees **Bryn** and **Chris**.*

TOM Bryn! Chris! Great!

*When **Tom** sees **Ruthlyn** and **Helen**, too late, he puts a restraining hand on **Chris's** arm, and their laughter freezes.*

*Ruthlyn goes off, **Tom** and **Bryn** run off.*

HELEN *facing Chris* Dear Nobody,
I hate him, I hate him, I hate him.

BRYN *enters and sits with her back to* **Chris** Dear Chris,
Why don't you answer my letters? It was lovely to see you
in Sheffield the other week. I'm so excited about going up
to Leeds, and you won't be that far away, will you, when
you're in Newcastle? Will you come and see me sometimes
– just for a laugh, eh? I miss you.

CHRIS 'I miss you,' she said. It hurt to read it. I could
hear her voice and her laugh in every word I read. I knew
it would never work the way she wanted it. There was
too much of me that was hurt, tied up in something that
I couldn't work out, never would work out, like the
threads of a spider's web that won't ever snap. So I wrote
to her.

BRYN *reading* Dear Bryn,
I like you very much. Please believe me. I'm sorry if this
will hurt you but I don't think things could ever work
between us. I don't think we should ever meet again.

Bryn and Helen go, then followed by Chris.

*Joan and Alan enter, separately, come towards each other
and kiss nervously and as strangers.*

They sit.

Chris enters.

JOAN Christopher! We've been waiting for you!

Unwillingly **Chris** *joins them.*

CHRIS So. My mother comes home, does she? Isn't it a bit
late! I could have done with you ten years ago.

DON Now Christopher, this is not an occasion for
bitterness.

JOAN And I haven't come home.

CHRIS Well! Let's celebrate the fact that you haven't come
home, eh Dad?

ALAN It's all right, Chris. It's all right. I invited Joan and
Don here. Your mother and I are getting a divorce.

JOAN *raising a glass* Our divorce.

CHRIS *ironic, hurting himself with his blurted-out
sarcasm. This is unlike him.* Well that's wonderful. And I
thought you did that years ago.

DON And Don and I are going to get married.

CHRIS   I thought you were already married. Or were you just practising?

ALAN   Drink, Chris. We're celebrating this together.

Chris shakes hands with them, not in the least bit celebrating with them, but with ironic courtesy, as if he is giving them permission to celebrate. He walks past them and hurls his glass, and over the sound effects come the exaggerated sound of glass splintering.

CHRIS   *shouting*   HELEN!

CHRIS   *to himself*   It was beautiful, the way that perfect shell burst apart and splintered; the way the stars of glass caught light and soared before they fell.

CHRIS   *talking to the audience*   It's strange how you can go for years and years letting other people be responsible for the way you think and dress and eat, what you learn, how you speak, and all of a sudden you find you've broken away from all that web of protection and you're spinning out into space, a free body.

Joan comes to stand by him.

JOAN   Christopher. Tell me about you and Helen.

CHRIS   I haven't spoken to Helen since the end of June.

JOAN   I gathered that. And can you put it all behind you?

CHRIS   Like hell I can.

JOAN   It'll get better, Christopher. It takes time, but it will get better.

He rejoins her and Alan.

CHRIS   I'm sorry. I was angry just now.

JOAN   It's all right. You had every right to be angry.

Don comes forward and puts his arm around her, and they go.

Alan and Chris stand apart in silence, then Alan comes slowly forward, touches Chris's shoulder, and they leave together.

Chris goes to his room.

HELEN   *goes to her room*   September 30th
Dear Nobody,
I feel peculiar tonight. Terrible. I can hardly walk in fact. You've moved right down. Dropped, the midwife said. Turned, and ready for action. I wish I was. God, I'm so fed up.

CHRIS   I wrote down a poem for Helen. It was something I'd learnt at school. It was the only kind of present I could give her.

He goes to her door, and stands face to face with **Ted**. **Helen** *is half-aware of him.*

TED   *embarrassed*   Hello Chris!

CHRIS   Hello, Mr Garton.

TED   Haven't seen you for a long time. How's the guitar coming on?

CHRIS   Fine.

TED   Looking forward to university, I expect.

CHRIS   How's Helen, Mr Garton?

TED   She's looking very large. Like a potato.

CHRIS   Could I see her, just for a minute?

TED   No . . . er . . . no, Chris. I'm afraid that wouldn't be . . .wouldn't be possible.

CHRIS   I'm going away the day after tomorrow. I just want to say goodbye to her. And to give her this.

TED   We don't want to upset her.

CHRIS   Please . . . could you just give her this from me?

TED   Well, I . . .

CHRIS   Please, Mr Garton. It's very important.

*Ted takes it and turns away. **Chris** backs away looking up at the house, then sits cross-legged, hugging himself, waiting.*

HELEN   September 30th
Later.
A few minutes ago, I felt a massive kind of cramp rising up from the base of my spine, right up, spreading out and up till it held me in the centre of it. It seemed to take hold of my whole body and when I felt I was going to burst with it it died away again. I'm not frightened. I know exactly what it is. It means you're coming. This is the last letter I will write to you.
She puts all the letters in a box.
Mum! Mum!

Alice runs in, flustered, and takes command of the situation.

HELEN   Mum, I think it's coming.

ALICE   *this is the first moment of tenderness between them.* Hold me, Helen. Come on, hold on tight.

HELEN   Mum! It hurts! It hurts.

ALICE   You're all right. You'll be all right. Hold on now. Hold on. Can you lie down?

HELEN   I think so.

ALICE   I'll go and phone the midwife. I'll come right back. Ted! *She goes.*   Keep an eye on her, will you?

Helen lies on the bed, not daring to move.

TED   *tiptoing in*   Helen?

HELEN   Dad.

TED   You'll be all right. The ambulance is coming, and your midwife's on her way round. Mum's just packing a bag.

HELEN   Thanks, Dad.

TED   Here, Helen. I think you should have this now. Chris brought it round for you. Your mother doesn't know.

He goes.

Helen takes the envelope from him and sits up. As she begins to read, Chris appears at side and they say it half-together.

CHRIS   Had I the heaven's embroidered cloths
Enwrought with gold and silver light,
The blue and the dim and the dark cloths
Of night and light and the half light,
I would spread the cloths under your feet:

HELEN   *joining in*   But I, being poor, have only my dreams;
I have spread my dreams under your feet;
Tread softly because you tread on my dreams.

HELEN   Oh, Chris! Chris!   *She's crying.*

Chris goes to side of stage.

TED   *enters*   Helen? Are you all right?

HELEN   Yes. I'm all right. Thanks Dad.

TED   Is there anything you want me to do?

HELEN   I want Chris to know . . . I think he should know, Dad.

TED   All right. I'll tell him, I promise.

HELEN   Dad – you wouldn't take him these, would you? It's just some letters. I want him to have them.

Ted sighs, confused.

TED   Well, your mother . . . I think she'd be very upset . . .

HELEN   Please Dad. I want him to have them before he goes away.

*Ted makes up his mind to take them. **Helen** bundles up the letters and at the same time as handing them to **Ted**, **Alan** comes to **Chris** and hands them to him.*

*Collage of quotes, spoken in canon by **Chris** and **Helen**:*
Dear Nobody, Dear Nobody, Nobody, Nobody, Nobody . . .
At home there's a tap that won't stop dripping . . .
Pregnant, pregnant, what if I'm pregnant . . . I want Chris to hold me in his arms and say it's all right, we'll manage . . . I hate him, I hate him, I hate him . . . I know exactly what it is. It means you're coming.

ALAN   Chris? Are you all right?

Helen shrieks.

CHRIS   The baby's coming! Let Helen be all right, oh let her be all right.

*Newborn baby cry. **Chris** runs off.*

Alan leaves separately.

*Ted and **Alice** stand by **Helen's** bed. **Helen** is propped up on pillows. **Alice** puts the shawl bundle into her arms.*

*Chris bursts in and **Ted** and **Alice** turn to look at him. He makes straight for **Helen**.*

HELEN   Chris. Look.

*All except **Chris** and **Helen** leave stage.*

CHRIS   *facing the audience*   I saw something that was tiny and red-faced, crinkled-up, sleeping, breathing, an unbelievable, still presence in the room.

*Blast of rock music to which **Tom** and **Ruthlyn** run on. Noise of train station.*

Helen lifts the baby out of its cradle.

RUTHLYN   *hugging **Tom***   Bye Tom. Have a great time at Newcastle, you swats!

TOM   See you at Christmas, Ruthlyn!

*Chris steps away from **Helen**, torn between the two, and joins **Tom**.*

RUTHLYN   Bye now, big Daddy!

She goes.

Noise of train.

TOM   Looking forward to it, Chris?

CHRIS   Mmm?

TOM The big break. The big world. We've left home! At last! We're free.

CHRIS I suppose we are.

TOM I've waited for this moment for eighteen years! The end of one chapter, the beginning of the next. Mine's a horror story, Chris. What's yours? *singing* Oh mamma, you'd better watch out – your little boy's a big boy now!

Sings and swaggers across stage and off.

Alice enters and she and Helen sit next to each other.

Chris moves to side of stage and begins to half write.

CHRIS Dear Amy,
This is your story. I don't know yet where it's going to end. Your name means 'Loved One', or 'Friend', and we both chose it. This is your story.

Nan comes into the room and looks at the baby. Helen smiles at her. Alice looks at her, unwelcoming. Nan sits down and watches them.

CHRIS When I saw you that day at the hospital I realised that during all those months of separation from Helen I hadn't thought once about you. You were nobody. It was Helen I was thinking about day and night, night and day. I wanted to be with her and to hold her. I wanted everything to be the same again. But when I saw her at last you were there.

Helen stoops to put the baby in the cradle, but Alice takes it from her, uncertain. She turns towards Nan.

CHRIS I was shocked by your importance, by your vulnerability. The thought of holding you or even touching you scared me, tiny creature that you were. I tried to look at you and say, she is ours, and I couldn't. I felt weak. I wanted to hide from you.

Alice hands the baby to Nan.

ALICE Here you are, Mum. Helen's baby. Would you like to hold her?

NAN I would, Alice. Do you know, she reminds me of you. She's a beautiful baby.

HELEN Dear Amy,
It is as though you are a fine thread being drawn through a garment, mending tears.

The three women are lit in a tableau group.

CHRIS Helen is right. I'm not ready for you, or for her. I'm not yet ready for myself.

STAGING THE PLAY

The play tells the story of two young people, Chris and his girlfriend Helen. During their A-level year, Helen becomes pregnant. The effect of that pregnancy both on Helen and Chris and on their friends and families is played out in a fast-moving, naturalistic drama.

The common thread linking the scenes is the narrative device of Helen's letters to the unborn child. This creates moments of quiet and reflection within the play as well as revealing Helen's inner turmoil. We learn about Chris from the letters he writes to his mother and from his romantic soliloquies. The play provides many opportunities for creative writing and drama work exploring the portrayal of emotions.

The settings for much of the action become clear only through what the actors do, for example, miming wading in a stream, horse-back riding and so on. Work will have to be done that encourages the actors' physicality and their ease in suggesting different locations through gesture and movement.

A simple proscenium arch setting could have Chris's bedroom upstage right, perhaps on a rostrum, the sitting room downstage right linked to the bedroom with a couple of steps and Helen's sitting-room downstage left. This will leave the centre of the stage clear to represent the moors, Chris's mother's house, the doctor's surgery, etc. Think about the ease with which furniture can be moved on and off. The use of simple visual representation can suggest many different scenes, for example, a hospital, using a screen or a bedside cabinet.

Set for a proscenium-style stage

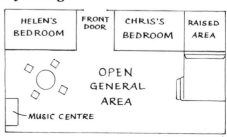

PROSCENIUM ARCH PLAN

HELEN'S BEDROOM | FRONT DOOR | CHRIS'S BEDROOM | RAISED AREA

OPEN GENERAL AREA

MUSIC CENTRE

In the round

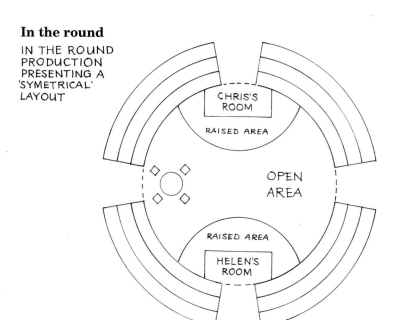

IN THE ROUND
PRODUCTION
PRESENTING A
'SYMETRICAL'
LAYOUT

CHRIS'S ROOM

RAISED AREA

OPEN AREA

RAISED AREA

HELEN'S ROOM

Consider a production in the round. This should have as few pieces of furniture as possible in order not to block the sightlines of the audience. A school hall may have features which can be incorporated into the play, for example, a balcony on which to set the scenes at the Leadmill, or wall-bars for the scene at the climbing-wall. Your audience will not mind turning in their seats to see action not taking place within the acting area, but bear in mind this will only be possible for short scenes.

Lighting

Apart from well-focused lighting for each of the individual areas, think about special effects that can be achieved through using coloured, 'disco' lighting for the scene at the Leadmill, or night lighting for Helen and Chris's walks on the moors. Stars are a recurring metaphor in the play, so a dramatic and moving effect can be achieved by hanging a 'starcloth' at the back of the stage. This can be done by making holes in a large piece of blackout material hanging at the back of the stage. Place floodlights on racks behind the cloth and 'box in' with flats at either end with the cloth's edges attached carefully to the flats so as not to allow any light to escape at the sides.

Music

Music is an important theme in this play. Helen's musical future is affected by her pregnancy; love of music is what bonds her and her father. If you do not have musical actors then the importance can be suggested with the use of an onstage hi-fi system to replace the piano. Another point at which music is necessary is to set the scenes at the Leadmill. Music can also be used to underscore dramatic moments, for example during Chris's soliloquies.

Sound Effects

These are few and far between but they are vital for heightening the dramatic tension. Consider whether the cast can create the sounds of horses galloping rather than having it on the sound-tape. Could this be more effective?

Costumes

Costumes should be kept simple. Basic casual clothes, jeans and T-shirts with jumpers and anoraks for the winter scenes, shorts for the holiday in France. Helen's developing pregnancy can be suggested by baggier clothing. Actual padding should not be needed until the very end, if at all, as it rarely looks convincing. The actress playing Helen should suggest the growing weight and discomfort by slower, heavier movement.

WORK ON AND AROUND THE SCRIPT

DRAMA

1 The Family Dynamic.

Organisation: In groups of three – Ted, Alice and Helen – work out what Helen's future might have been if she had not got pregnant.

Situation: Alice, Helen's mother seems opposed to her going to music school. What are her mother's ambitions for her in contrast to Helen's hopes and her father's plans?

First Line: ALICE: Music is such an uncertain profession, Helen. This is your whole future you're deciding here.

---

2 What Happened to Chris's mum?

Organisation: Work in groups of four or five – Chris, his parents and a friend or friends.

Situation: The ten-year-old Chris overhears the scene where his mum leaves his father. He then confides what has happened to a friend. What does he understand of what he has heard? How does he communicate his understandings to his friend?

First Line: JOAN: This is very hard for me. I've thought it through and I can't take Chris with me.

---

3 Looking Before You Leap.

Organisation: In pairs.

Situation: Chris and his dad have a man-to-man talk. How easy is it for Chris to confide in his father? Can Alan talk freely to his son?

First Line: ALAN: You and Helen seem very close. I hope you're being sensible.

---

4 Confiding.

Organisation: In pairs.

Situation: In the play Helen does not confide in Ruthlyn until near the end of her pregnancy. Why is that?
First Line: RUTHLYN: I don't believe it. Not you, Helen, you're such a goody-two-shoes.

---

5 Practicalities.

Organisation: In threes. Doctor, Alice and Helen.

Situation: The pregnancy is discussed with Alice being a little more rational, but still bitterly opposed to Helen keeping the baby.

First Line: DOCTOR: I'll put her forward for a termination if that's what she wants, but I wonder if you've considered all the options.

---

6 Trapped.

Organisation: In a large group create a nightmare sequence, maybe taking as a starting point the horse-riding scene. Helen is re-living this incident in her dreams, with Chris and members of her family appearing as part of it. Remember that dreams take on an exaggerated quality. Use distorted sounds and movements to create a nightmare effect. Share your nightmare with the rest of the class.

---

7 Abandoned.

Organisation: In pairs, one person takes on the role of Joan, Chris's mother and the other is Don, her new boyfriend.

Situation: The play provides several different examples of mothers. Chris's mother is unusual in that she leaves home without taking her son. Explore her reasons and consider how much influence her boyfriend Don might have had on her behaviour.

First Line: DON: Come on, Joan, we talked about this. How are photography, mountaineering and a ten-year old child going to mix?

---

8 Across the generations.

Organisation: In threes. Helen, Alice and Nan.

Situation: At the end of the play it is suggested that Nan and Alice are somehow united by the birth of Amy. What do you think they are saying to each other as the curtain falls?

First Line: ALICE: Here, Mum. Would you like to hold her?

---

9 The Future.

Organisation: In threes. Helen, Chris and the now teenage Amy.

Situation: Helen and Chris are advising Amy, who has become seriously involved with a boyfriend. What do they tell her about their own past? How would they handle it?

First Line: AMY: I'm really fond of Mike, Mum. We're thinking of going on holiday together.

---

10 Chris's future.

Organisation: In mixed pairs. Chris and his new girlfriend have been together a while.

Situation: They have been together about five years and Bryn is keen to start a family. How much does Chris tell her about the past? How does it affect his feelings now?

First Line: CHRIS: Look, Bryn, I know you're keen to have a baby but I'm really not sure.

Movement

1. Create a series of tableaux showing a family as it develops. Include babies, toddlers, schoolchildren, etc. and show different relationships and dependencies as the adults rearrange themselves and grow progressively older in each successive tableau.

2. Try walking across the room showing an increase in age from the present to old age. Now try again from a pre-walking stage. Remember not to exaggerate the effects of age. Elderly people may move somewhat slowly and stiffly, but they are seldom actually bent double or tottering.

3. Look at the moments in the play where it would be possible to integrate some dance/drama. For example, try creating a 'living wall' for Chris to climb, in the scene at the end of Act 1.

4. Using the nightmare exercise, (see 6 above) discover what movement elements could be incorporated to make the horse-riding scene more effective.

5. Collect information from people you know who have had babies, about the changes that advancing pregnancy makes in the way you stand and move. Use these ideas to help with the depiction of Helen.

Written work

1. Write a 500-word review of the play as if you'd just seen it performed. Attempt to give your readers a clear idea of the themes, characters and dramatic action.

2. Write a 60-second TV trailer as if the play were going to be televised. Write a powerful, succinct linking narrative with highlights from the scenes within the play. Which aspects of the play do you need to consider when choosing what to focus on in a limited time?

3. Write Helen's diary entry for the birth of Amy.

4. Write a letter from Chris telling his mother about Helen and the baby and his feelings and plans for the future.

FROM NOVEL TO PLAY

Berlie Doherty gives us a clear insight into Helen's family background in her novel, *Dear Nobody*.

Read the following extract from the book.

And because she sat there, so still and shocked, sipping at an empty sherry glass, I asked, brave as anything, Nobody, if I was born before she was married. She closed her eyes and shuddered, as if she was suddenly cold to the bone. We could hear Robbie outside, singing as he was digging. He would be so hot, out there. Any minute now he'd come in for water and would flop on the settee, legs sprawled out in front of him, staring from one to the other of us, knowing he was missing something. Somewhere in the room a bluebottle was buzzing. I think it was trapped in the curtains.

Mum said no, of course not, they'd been married for two years before I was born. She picked up a letter that was lying on the table in front of her and started fanning herself with it. "This dreadful heat," she said.

I was a dog on the scent now, digging away, sending all the muck flying up. "But there was a baby, wasn't there? Nan said. 'Like mother, like daughter .' What did she mean?"

I had to find out, Nobody, for you. It seemed to be part of your past, and part of our future.

"If it wasn't me, who was it? Where is it now?"

She said it was none of my business, and calm as anything, feeling that deep inside I was the same person as she was, just as you're the same person I am, just as she is the same person as that quiet, sad old woman staring all day and all life out of a crack in her bedroom curtains, I told her that I thought it *was* my business.

"What are you trying to ask me, Helen?" she said at last, and I told her that from what my nan had said it sounded as if I'd been born illegitimate. I was sure that was what she had meant. I told her the words: "bad blood". It was a hard thing to say. "Like mother, like daughter." I was hurting myself, too. I was hurting you.

"Do you imagine I'd do a thing like that?" she said then, her voice gone cold and shaking. "A dirty thing like that?"

No. After all I couldn't imagine it. Not if she thought it was dirty. How can love be dirty? If she'd said sinful, or silly, or thoughtless, it wouldn't have hurt so much as that word "dirty" did. For a minute I was sidetracked. I asked her if she'd ever been in love, then, which I suppose was a bit of an impertinence. But she's so difficult to talk to. She's such a closed-up, tight woman at times. I can't imagine her being the same age as me, ever. She won't give anything, just as she won't take anything from me.

"Well. Were you in love with Dad when you married him?" Why couldn't she answer that, at least, instead of sitting there with her mouth all pursed up, fanning herself with her eyes closed, locked away from me? I wanted to see Alice, the girl that she was, the me in her at eighteen or so. And she couldn't answer that question, or wouldn't. Does that mean she did or she didn't? I remembered Mum then as she used to be when I was a kid, at Christmas time perhaps when she'd had a drink or two. I remembered watching her once, shimmying round the kitchen in an odd, flappy dance that had made Robbie and me laugh. My dad was watching her, too, in a half-proud, half-disapproving way, and she had danced up to him and put both her hands on his shoulders and danced just for him, holding his eyes in hers, and both of them gone quiet as night, till

I'd felt embarrassed and locked out. Things like that didn't happen any more.

And then, just when I'd given up and I was about to go out of the room she said, "If you must know, Helen, I'm the one who's illegitimate, not you."

The bluebottle had gone still. Even Robbie had stopped his maniac singing. "I was born out of wedlock, as they say. Born in sin. And I'll never forgive my mother for that."

That was when the talking started, little Nobody.

"I don't know who my father is, " she said. "Except, Helen, that he was a dancer in a night-club. It was your father who found that out."

I was utterly shocked at this news. I walked over to the the window and watched Robbie at his digging. One of his friends had come round to help him. They'd stripped off their tee-shirts. I could see how their shoulders were looking pink and sore already.

"So Grandad isn't really..." I couldn't take it in. I felt closer to my grandfather than to any other member of my family; always had done.

"He married her when I was about nine. And that, I can tell you, was a brave and generous thing to do. In those days an unmarried mother was no more than a slut. Her child was a disgrace. My mother's family wouldn't own her. She was an outcast, and so was I. A bastard, that's what you were called if you didn't have a father. That's what I was called, when I was a child at school. That's the start I had in life."

It was as if she'd taken all the guilt of it on herself, all the family shame, and tried to put things right all through her life. I understood her then, for the first time in my life. I understood her commitment to that word "decency" which was a word she cradled as if it was a gem, a precious legacy from another age. I was more shocked and confused by all this than if she'd told me what I'd thought had been the case, that I was born before she was married, or that she'd had a baby before she had me, or anything like that.

Because what she was telling me was something that she'd had no choice about, and that she wished had never happened. We have no choice about being born, little Nobody. I've made up your mind for you.

It's not a stigma any more, not like it was when Mum was a child. No one will be calling you names.

But I hope you'll forgive me just the same.

- What information do we get from this extract about the family background that we don't get in the playscript?

- Which member of the family do you feel most sympathy for? Grandad, Nan or Alice? Why?

- Create a series of tableaux that would illustrate the background to Nan's and Alice's lives, for example:

  1. Nan meeting Alice's father at the dance.

  2. Alice at school.

  3. Grandad becoming one of the family.

Add any other tableaux that you think would be appropriate.

THEMES IN AND AROUND THE PLAY

CHILDHOOD

The play contains Nan's powerful account of her childhood.
This is because one of the play's main themes is the transition
from childhood to adulthood; the point is that to be truly adult
often means becoming responsible for someone else's
childhood.

Drama

In groups, each take a different character, Helen, Chris,
Ruthlyn, Alice, Ted, Alan or Joan. Invent a childhood for each
one, which is delivered as a monologue to the rest of the
group. It can focus on one revealing or traumatic incident, or
be a general picture of life as a child. Use the information
contained in the play to help you.

■ AUTOBIOGRAPHY

In my childhood trees were green
And there was plenty to be seen.

Come back early or never come.

My father made the walls resound,
He wore his collar the wrong way round.

Come back early or never come.

My mother wore a yellow dress:
Gently, gently, gentleness.

Come back early or never come.

When I was five the black dreams came;
Nothing after was quite the same.

Come back early or never come.

The dark was talking to the dead;
The lamp was dark beside my bed.

Come back early or never come.

When I woke they did not care:
Nobody, nobody was there.

Come back early or never come.

When my silent terror cried,
Nobody, nobody replied.

Come back early or never come.

I got up; the chilly sun
Saw me walk alone.

Come back early or never come.

Louis MacNeice, *The Rattlebag Anthology* **Faber & Faber 1982**

- In a group, read through this poem. Try dividing up the lines among the group and speaking the refrain in a chorus to heighten the rhythm and drama of the lines.

- Discuss what experience or experiences the poem might be about. How might they affect the child's future behaviour? Why do you think the poem is called *Autobiography*?

- Write a short story that might explain the images in the poem.

■ PREGNANCY: FACT AND FICTION

1989 -1992

Number of births outside marriage
1981   **91,300**
1991   **236,100**

Total percentage of all live births
1981   **12.5**
1991   **29.8**

Deaths in the first year of life per 1,000
1980
Marital   **12.2**
Non-marital   **16.4**

Number of one-parent families
1980
940,000
1 in 8 families
1.5 million children

1992
1.3 million
1 in 5 families
2.1 million children

From the Workhouse to the Workplace **NCOPF**

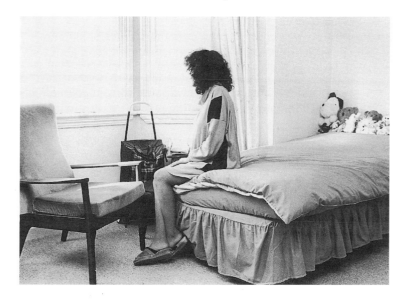

Discussion

1 There is no suggestion in the play that Helen and Chris thought about the possibility of pregnancy when they made love. Why do you think this was the case? Were they too embarrassed to discuss the matter? Perhaps they thought that pregnancy couldn't occur the first time they had sex.

2 In small groups, write down all the 'old wives' tales you know about avoiding pregnancy. Share these with the other groups. Now all together draw up a list of all the methods of contraception you are aware of. Write them in descending order, from most effective to least effective.

3 Get in touch with the agencies at the end of this material and ask them to send you contraception information packs and check how accurate you were.

4 If you could plan a course in sex education for your school what would you like it to contain? How would you like the lessons organised? Should boys and girls be taught separately and should they be taught different things?

Drama

• Work in pairs. Imagine that one of you might be pregnant and the other is putting the case for a termination. The pairs might be parent and daughter, two friends or boyfriend and girlfriend.

• Run the scene twice; first with the persuader being angry and domineering, and the second time being loving and kind.

• Try the same situation again, swapping roles if you like, but this time the persuader is arguing against a termination.

MOTHER AND BABY IMAGES

Look at the picture of a mother and baby.

Write a list of words to describe the picture. Share all the words with the rest of the group. Now try to grade them into positive and negative lists.

Divide into single gender groups. Using magazines, newspapers, glue and scissors, cut out pictures which show images of young men (for the male students' group) and young women (for the female students' group) and make a collage entitled 'How We Are Meant To Be'.

In a mixed group discuss how accurate these images are. Do they put you under pressure to look or behave a certain way? Are they useful in helping you decide what sort of person to be? Why are certain images more prevalent than others? Who decides on these images and controls them and why?

PARENTING

Discussion

The female students in the group imagine that they are in the same position as Helen. Draw up a list on one half of a piece of paper of all the things Helen might miss out on by having the baby, and on the other half, all the things she will gain.

The male students do the same exercise as if they were considering the situation from Chris's point of view.

Share the lists. Start with the negative things and then share the positive aspects. Are the lists similar?

Now both groups should try the same exercise from the point of view of Chris and Helen as if they had decided to stay together. How much responsibility will they share? What problems are solved by being together? Could any problems be created by being together?

The Egg Exercise

Select an Egg Midwife (male or female). He or she will be responsible for the issuing of fresh eggs to everyone in the group at the start of the week.

You must keep your egg warm, dry and safe at all times. You must always have it in your sight and if you go anywhere or do anything where it is not possible to include the egg, you must arrange 'eggsitting', and either pay a fee or in turn provide reciprocal 'eggsitting'.

Keep a diary of the egg's care and comfort for the week.

If an egg breaks, a two-day period of mourning will be observed and a fine will be paid, after which time the Midwife will issue a new egg.

At the end of the week, share your diary and your thoughts and feelings on how the egg affected your activities with the rest of the group. If some of you were unable to care for your eggs, find out why and discuss the problems.

Written Work

The facts

- Adoption has been legally recognised in Britain since the 1920s.

- There have been nearly 1 million adoptions since then.

- It is estimated that around 50 per cent of all adoptions are step-parent adoptions.

- Adopting a child in the UK is free.

- For every child offered for adoption in the UK there are thought to be 10 adoptive parents waiting.

- Adopting a child from overseas can cost £10,000 and take six months.

- In the United States there are some 500 contested adoptions every year – when parents who have given up their children for adoption change their minds.

- After 1989, foreigners took out many babies and children, prompting the Romanian government to begin controlling the practice. At present the Romanian authorities are only offering children with special needs.

- Until 1967 the British government encouraged agencies to send children to the colonies for adoption, cutting them off from their families. Between 1882 and 1935, Barnados sent 30,000 boys and girls to Canada; between 1921 and 1967, it sent 3,400 to Australia.

The Guardian August 30 1994

Children about to set sail for Australia in 1948.

In small groups write a questionnaire that might be set by an adoption agency for completion by prospective parents.

What facts would it be important to discover? Consider how questions should be phrased in order to establish someone's grasp of the financial, moral and emotional issues involved.

Pool your work to produce a definitive questionnaire. Limit it to two sides of A4.

In mixed pairs, complete the questionnaire.

Drama

1 In threes. One is from the adoption agency and the other two are prospective parents. Conduct an interview based on the responses to the questionnaire. The interviewer must assess the suitability of the would-be parents. Show your scene to the rest of the group. Discuss how the interviewers and interviewees handled the situation. Will they make suitable parents?

2 Again, work in threes. Two parents and a young person they are thinking of adopting from a children's home. Set the situation for a first meeting. Consider their different backgrounds and what they all want from each other.

3 The same people, six months later. The young person has been living with them for some months and has been discovered smoking by the parents. How do they handle it?

WHO IS RESPONSIBLE?

Read the following piece.

Irresponsible Teenager

Currently expecting a child with another woman, 19-year-old Adrian (not his real name) is not in touch with the mother of his two-year-old son. He lives with his mother and stepfather in Crystal Palace, London, works as a part-time despatch rider and does occasional decorating for friends.

‘When I first found I was going to be a father, I was just 17 and couldn't help feeling secretly proud, even though I told the girl I didn't want to know about it. I fed her the "How do I know it's mine?" line like mates told me to, even though I knew, deep down, there was nobody else who could have been the father. She and I had been having sex on and off for a year and she wasn't the sort of girl to go off with anyone else. She was really crazy over me, and threw herself at me from the start even though I wasn't that keen, so I reckoned it was as much her fault as mine.

I never saw that baby. Luckily my parents separated at that time so I made myself scarce and went to live with my dad in the Midlands for a while. Apparently her parents kicked up a stink and went round to my mum's house demanding I face up to my responsibilities, but my mum sent them packing saying their daughter was a tried and tested slag and that it wasn't my kid and, even if it was, I was a lost cause like my father.

I still talk about it now with a sense of pride. I hear myself saying to people who know my ex-girlfriend, who's having my second kid later this year, "I am already a dad, I was a dad at 17." It gives me street cred.

The girl who's having my second kid got pregnant even though we took precautions. You can never trust girls these days. We had an accident with a condom and she said she'd go to the doctor about the morning-after pill.

It turned out she didn't because one of her friends told her it makes you throw up all night and she was due to go on holiday the day after. She took

79

a chance and was unlucky. Again, I don't feel in any way responsible. We used contraception. It failed and she didn't get it sorted out. I made it quite plain to her I was not interested in a baby at 19 and she had plenty of time to do something about it.

As it is, I feel my first responsibility is to myself. I've got to get my life sorted out, get a steady job, move out of home eventually and make a good living. Having kids would be a real grind and would have made me the miserable uptight sort of man you see in old 1960s films who got a girl pregnant in his teens and spent the rest of his life trying to play happy families.

Of course I am actually going to see my next kid when it's born later this year. I keep in touch with my ex-girlfriend because of that. I won't be there at the birth or signing birth certificates at the town hall, but I'll probably pitch up when she's back home and have a look. I do sometimes think about my first child and I'd like at least to see this one, if only to see whether it looks like me. I don't intend to actually spend any time with it though, that's Child Support Agency land and I want to keep well clear of them.

Am I irresponsible? My mum says so, but I intend to settle down and get married and have kids one day and then I'll make up for lost time. I think, given the right circumstances, I'd be a good dad. I don't feel guilty about having fathered the two children I have, because of the world we live in now.

It's every man for himself now and besides, the girls are hardly going to be thrown out in the streets to starve like the little match girl, are they? They are no longer social lepers, unmarried mums.

Someone will take care of them, whether it's their parents, new blokes or the state, so there's no need to feel guilty. **,**

The Sunday Times 3 July 1994

- What are Adrian's attitudes towards women? Where does he get these beliefs from – his own experiences, his friends' views, the media?

- His mother calls his girlfriend a 'slag'. Can this term be applied to boys? Do girls admire boys who are sexually promiscuous?

- Should he be involved in the future of his children?

- What should their mother tell them about him?

UNMARRIED MOTHER

In 1993, a government minister suggested that young unmarried girls deliberately become pregnant in order to qualify for council housing. How accurate do you think this is? What image of single mothers do we get from the media?

Read the following extract.

As the child became more demanding, Lizzie became more silent. Some days, Christie could hardly get a word from her lips. Once or twice she stayed away a whole day and night and Christie coped as best he could with the nappies and bottles. He dredged his memory for songs to sing the child to sleep and surprised himself with the vast catalogue stored in his subconscious. He no longer fretted about getting old; the coming of Liam had taken decades off his age and filled his life with meaning.

The opposite seemed to be true for Lizzie. She grew paler by the week, she hardly ate anything and slept most of the day. In the end, Christie asked Mrs Cahill to call and see if anything could be done. She arrived, laden with home-made bread and preserves and spent a good part of three hours sitting in Lizzie's room. Every so often she came out to refill the teapot, but revealed nothing to Christie except for raising her right eyebrow occasionally. Liam and Christie played and walked and talked and eventually fell asleep on one another.

Mrs Cahill woke Christie as she lifted Liam into his cot. Lizzie was sleeping, she said with a sigh, then placed his hands around a mug of amber tea. She sat across from him and the two of them, unspeaking for a moment, looked more like fireplace ornaments than living people.

"What's to be done?" he asked after a while.

"Ah sure I've seen it before dear. You'd be surprised how often. Some girls can be persuaded to carry on, but they're never truly happy, Christie love. There's only one cure for Lizzie, "Mrs Cahill said.

"And what would that be?" he asked.

"She must be allowed to go, and leave the child behind, or very soon she will die anyway," Mrs Cahill said quietly.

Christie was amazed at her words, but he knew her as woman of strength and conviction who would never make light of so grave a matter. His main surprise came from the newly-acquired knowledge that women were prepared to die rather than be burdened with children. It was an alien idea to grasp, but accept it he did.

Lizzie left the day after Liam's first birthday, the colour back in her cheeks and a smile on her lips. Christie bought her a boat ticket to England. She sailed from Dublin to Liverpool in November 1928. Christie received a letter from her in the New Year. It bore a street name but no number, and was barely literate. It was the last time she wrote.

The Common Thread, by **Kitty Fitzgerald, Mandarin**

- Why does Lizzie leave her baby? Is she a 'bad mother'?
- What is Christie's role? Is he able to cope? What qualities does he have that the baby's mother doesn't?
- Should a child always be brought up by its natural parents whatever the circumstances?

TV

In groups, plan a TV documentary on the subject of young unmarried mothers. Decide on who you will need to interview and what point you are trying to make. If you have access to a camcorder, actually create the documentary with members of the group playing single mothers, single fathers, government representatives, health officials, teachers, and so on.

Problems

Write a problem page of letters and answers to some of the things you have discovered and discussed in your work on the themes of *Dear Nobody*.

HISTORICAL ATTITUDES

Life for the unmarried mother in 1918 was fraught with difficulty and hardship and the death-rate for children born outside marriage was twice that of other children. The state gave no financial support to unmarried mothers other than subsistence within the workhouse. While widows and the separated were given small sums to allow them to remain in the community, the unmarried mother and her child faced a life of destitution in the workhouse, children and mothers living separately in large dormitories. Many women spent years in the workhouse as they were not allowed to leave until they could support themselves and their children outside; meanwhile many of the children died for lack of proper nutrition and care. Other babies died at the hands of their own mothers who were driven to infanticide by the impossibility of their situations and the need to conceal the birth.

For most unmarried mothers the alternatives to the workhouse were either a situation in domestic service where they would be allowed to keep their child or alternative employment and the boarding out of their child. The National Council for the Unmarried Mother and Her Child, as the National Council for One Parent Families was originally called, ran an employment agency to place lone parents in work, but there were many difficulties. Few employers of domestic servants were willing to accept a child and boarding out was very expensive for someone on a low wage. In addition the standard of care, particularly because of the lack of breast-feeding and poor hygiene, often constituted a danger to the child.

To prevent the separation of the mother and child, the Council set up homes where babies could be breast-fed for the first few months of life. It campaigned for an increase in the size of maintenance orders and sought to reform the law (the Bastardy Act) in order to reduce the legal distinction between marital and non-marital children.

Extract from *'From the Workhouse to the Workplace. 75 years of one-parent family life 1918–1993'* **by Hilary Macaskill, NCOPF**

A baby, only a few weeks old, was found at an exit of a cinema in Tottenham Court Road in the 1930s and taken in by the Marylebone Institution. Abandoned babies were often the result of the unmarried mother's desperate situation.

In the 1920s, unmarried women who had children were sometimes judged to be insane and put in asylums. In 1971, three elderly women were discovered to have been incarcerated for more than 50 years in mental homes for no other reason than that of having given birth to a baby while unmarried.

Research

Talk to an older friend or relative and collect some biographical detail, including memories of earlier social values and attitudes towards unmarried mothers. Research the subject in the school or local library. Present your findings to the rest of the group, either as a single case history or as a general picture. Focus on any period of history that interests you.

LITERATURE

Tess of the D'Urbervilles **by Thomas Hardy**

Tess is a peasant girl living in Dorset in the 1880s. She becomes pregnant as a result of a forceful seduction by a man from a higher position in society.

Read the following extract.

The infant's breathing grew more difficult, and the mother's mental tension increased. It was useless to devour the little thing with kisses; she could stay in bed no longer, and walked feverishly about the room.

"Oh merciful God, have pity; have pity upon my poor baby!" she cried. "Heap as much anger as you want to upon me, and welcome; but pity the child!"

She leant against the chest of drawers, and murmured incoherent supplications for a long while, till she suddenly started up.

"Ah! perhaps baby can be saved! Perhaps it will be just the same!"

She spoke so brightly that it seemed as though her face might have shone in the gloom surrounding her.

She lit a candle, and went to a second and a third bed under the wall, where she awoke her young sisters and brothers, all of whom occupied the same room. Pulling out the washing-stand so that she could get behind it, she poured some water from a jug, and made them kneel around, putting their hands together with fingers exactly vertical. While the children, scarcely awake, awe-stricken at her manner, their eyes growing larger and larger, remained in this position, she took the baby from her bed – a child's child – so immature as scarce to seem a sufficient personality to endow its producer with the maternal title. Tess then stood erect with the infant on her arm beside the basin, the next sister held the Prayer-Book open before her, as the clerk at church held it before the parson; and thus the girl set about baptizing her child.

Her figure looked singularly tall and imposing as she stood in her long white nightgown, a thick cable of twisted dark hair hanging straight down her back to her waist. The kindly dimness of the weak candle abstracted from her form and features the little blemishes which sunlight might have revealed – the stubble scratches upon her wrists, and the weariness of her eyes – her high enthusiasm having a transfiguring effect upon the face which had been her undoing, showing it as a thing of immaculate beauty, with a touch of dignity which was almost regal. The little ones kneeling round, their sleepy eyes blinking and red, awaited her preparations full of a suspended wonder which their physical heaviness at that hour would not allow to become active.

The most impressed of them said:

"Be you really going to christen him, Tess?"

The girl-mother replied in a grave affirmative.

"What's his name going to be?"

She had not thought of that, but a name suggested by a phrase in the book of Genesis came into her head as she proceeded with the baptismal service, and now she pronounced it:

"Sorrow, I baptize thee in the name of the Father, and of the Son, and of the Holy Ghost."

She sprinkled the water, and there was a silence.

"Say 'Amen', children."

The tiny voices piped in obedient response "Amen!"

Tess went on:

"We receive this child" – and so forth – "and do sign him with the sign of the Cross."

Here she dipped her hand into the basin, and fervently drew an immense cross upon the baby with her forefinger, continuing with the customary sentences as to his manfully fighting against sin, the world, and the devil, and being a faithful soldier and servant unto his life's end. She duly went on with the Lord's Prayer, the children lisping it after her in a thin, gnat-like wail, till, at the conclusion, raising their voices to clerk's pitch, they again piped into the silence, "Amen!"

Then their sister, with much augmented confidence in the efficacy of this sacrament, poured forth from the bottom of her heart the thanksgiving that follows, uttering it boldly and

triumphantly in the stopt-diapason note when her heart was in her speech, and which will never be forgotten by those who knew her. The ecstasy of faith almost apotheosized her; it set upon her face a glowing irradiation, and brought a red spot into the middle of each cheek; while the miniature candle-flame inverted in her eye-pupils shone like a diamond. The children gazed up at her with more and more reverence, and no longer had a will for questioning. She did not look like Sissy to them now, but as a being large, towering and awful – a divine personage with whom they had nothing in common.

Poor Sorrow's campaign against sin, the world, and the devil was doomed to be of limited brilliancy – luckily perhaps for himself, considering his beginnings. In the blue of the morning that fragile soldier and servant breathed his last and when the other children awoke they cried bitterly, and begged Sissy to have another pretty baby.

The calmness which had possessed Tess since the christening remained with her in the infant's loss. In the daylight, indeed, she felt her terrors about his soul to have been somewhat exaggerated; whether well founded or not she had no uneasiness now, reasoning that if Providence would not ratify such an act of approximation she, for one, did not value the kind of heaven lost by the irregularity – either for herself or for her child.

So passed away Sorrow the Undesired – that intrusive creature, that bastard gift of shameless Nature who respects not the social law; a waif to whom eternal Time had been a matter of days merely, who knew not that such things as years and centuries ever were; to whom the cottage interior was the universe, the week's weather climate, new-born babyhood human existence, and the instinct to suck human knowledge.

- Discuss the conflict in Tess between the pity she feels for her child and the shame she has in its existence.

- Could such a situation exist today?

- Rewrite the scene as part of a play. Alter or add to the dialogue if need be and put in the stage directions.

- Investigate the attitudes among other cultures to premarital sex. What are the consequences and/or punishments for men and women in other societies?

A *Taste Of Honey* by **Shelagh Delaney**

A *Taste Of Honey* was written when Shelagh Delaney was
eighteen. It is set in Salford, Manchester in the late 1950s.
Jo, a young girl, has been brought up solely by her mother.
She becomes pregnant after a short affair with a black sailor.
At this point in the play she has left home because of her
mother's recent marriage to a man called Peter, and is
sharing a ramshackle flat with a gay friend, Geof. Geof's
concern for Jo has led him to try to reconcile her with her
mother, Helen.

HELEN: Well, where's the lady in question?

GEOF: In there.

HELEN: What, lazing in bed, as usual? Come on, get up;
plenty of girls in your condition have to go out to work
and take care of a family. Come on, get up.

JO: What blew you in?

HELEN: Let's have a look at you.

JO: Who told you about me?

HELEN: Nobody.

JO: How did you get to know then?

HELEN: Come on, aren't you going to introduce me to your
boyfriend? Who is he?

JO: My boyfriend. Oh it's all right, we're so decent we're
almost dead. I said who told you about me?

HELEN: Does it matter?

JO: I told you to keep out of my affairs, Geoffrey. I'm not
having anybody running my life for me. What do you
think you're running? A 'Back to Mother' movement?

GEOF: Your mother has a right to know.

JO: She's got no rights where I'm concerned.

HELEN: Oh, leave him alone. You're living off him, by all
accounts.

JO: Who've you been talking to? That old hag downstairs?

HELEN: I didn't need to talk to her. The whole district
knows what's been going on here.

JO: And what has been going on?

HELEN: I suppose you think you can hide yourself away in
this chicken run, don't you? Well, you can't. Everybody
knows.

GEOF: She won't go out anywhere, not even for a walk and a bit of fresh air. That's why I came to you.

HELEN: And what do you think I can do about it? In any case, bearing a child doesn't place one under an obligation to it.

GEOF: I should have thought it did.

HELEN: Well, you've got another think coming. If she won't take care of herself that's her lookout. And don't stand there looking as if it's my fault.

GEOF: It's your grandchild.

HELEN: Oh, shut up, you put years on me. Anyway, I'm having nothing to do with it. She's more than I can cope with, always has been.

GEOF: That's obvious.

HELEN: And what's your part in this little Victorian Melodrama? Nursemaid?

JO: Serves you right for bringing her here, Geof.

HELEN: It's a funny-looking set-up to me.

JO: It's our business.

HELEN: Then don't bring me into it. Where's the loving father? Distinguished by his absence I suppose?

JO: That's right.

HELEN [to Geof]: Did she hear any more of him?

JO: No, she didn't.

HELEN: When I'm talking to the organ grinder I don't expect the monkey to answer.

JO: I could get him back tomorrow if I wanted to.

HELEN: Well, that's nice to know. He certainly left you a nice Christmas box. It did happen at Christmas, I suppose? When the cat's away.

GEOF: You've been away a long time.

HELEN: Oh, you shut up. Sling your hook!

JO: Will you keep out of this, Geoffrey?

HELEN: Well, come on, let's have a look at you. [Jo turns away.]
What's up? We're all made the same aren't we?

JO: Yes we are.

HELEN: Well then. Can you cut the bread on it yet? [Jo turns.]
Yes you're carrying it a bit high, aren't you? Are you going to the clinic regularly? Is she working?

GEOF: No, I told you, she doesn't like people looking at her.

HELEN: Do you think that people have got nothing better to do than look at you?

JO: Leave me alone.

HELEN: She'd be better off working than living off you like a little bloodsucker.

GEOF: She doesn't live off me.

JO: No, we share everything, see! We're communists too.

HELEN: That's his influence I suppose.

JO: Get out of here. I won't go out if I don't want to. It's nothing to do with you. Get back to you fancy man or your husband, or whatever you like to call him.

[Helen begins to chase her]

Aren't you afraid he'll run off and leave you if you let him out of your sight?

HELEN: I'll give you such a bloody good hiding in a minute, if you're not careful. That's what you've gone short of!

JO: Don't show yourself up for what you are!

HELEN: You couldn't wait, could you? Now look at the mess you've landed yourself in.

JO: I'll get out of it, without your help.

HELEN: You had to throw yourself at the first man you met, didn't you?

JO: Yes, I did, that's right.

HELEN: You're man mad.

JO: I'm like you.

HELEN: You know what they're calling you round here? A silly little whore!

JO: Well they all know where I get it from too.

HELEN: Let me get hold of her! I'll knock her bloody head round!

JO: You should have been locked up years ago, with my father.

HELEN: Let me get hold of her!

GEOF: Please, Jo, Helen, Jo, please!

HELEN: I should have got rid of you before you were born.

JO: I wish you had done. You did with plenty of others, I know.

HELEN: I'll kill her. I'll knock the living daylights out of her.

GEOF: Helen, stop it, you will kill her!

JO: If you don't get out of here I'll...jump out of the
  window.

  [There is a sudden lull]

GEOF: [Yelling:] Will you stop shouting, you two?

HELEN: We enjoy it.

GEOF: Helen!

HELEN: Now you're going to listen to a few home truths,
  my girl.

JO: We've had enough home truths!

HELEN: All right, you thought you knew it all before,
  didn't you? But you came a cropper, Now it's "poor
  little Josephine, the tragedy queen, hasn't life been
  hard on her". Well you fell down, you get up...
  nobody else is going to carry you about. Oh, I know
  you've got this pansified little freak to lean on, but
  what good will that do you?

JO: Leave Geof out of it!

HELEN: Have you got your breath back? Because there's some more I've got to get off my chest first.

JO: You don't half like the sound of your own voice.

GEOF: If I'd known you were going to bully her like this I'd never have asked you to come here.

HELEN: You can clear off! Take your simpering little face out of it!

JO: Yes, buzz off Geof! Well, who brought her here? I told you what sort of a woman she was. Go and... go and make a cup of tea.

[He goes]

Discussion

- Contrast the relationship between Jo and her mother with Helen in *Dear Nobody* and her mother.

- What characterises this mother/daughter relationship? How satisfactory is it from either side?

- Why do you think the author created the character of Geof?

Drama

- In groups of three, rehearse the scene and play it through for the rest of the group. Think about the humour in the play. Could it be rewritten for a more modern setting?

■ THE LULLABY

When she had the abortion
she didn't tell me.

she took a taxi to the clinic,
signed her name,
and waited with the other women
and one young girl who was sobbing,

that night she told me
she was tired.

She went to bed early
and turned on the fan –

its music helped her sleep –
and through its blades she heard me

singing
as I washed and put away the dishes.

Richard Jones, *The Virago Book of Birth Poetry*, **1993**

- How do you think the man found out about the abortion?

- What are his feelings about it?

- What do you imagine the woman's feelings are?

- Write a poem about the experience from her point of view.

■ PREGNANT TEENAGER ON THE BEACH

From her pool in the muddy shallows
she squints sixty yards out
at the white blister of the sunning deck
On the diving board
a girl her own age shrieks,
topples with a bronzed youth
into the green water.
Separately they rise, an arc of light
like a rapier between them.
Laughing,
their glances fence,
lock.

Before her, in water low as their knees,
a circle of mothers
tow children on inflated plastic ducks,

sprinkle the murky water
over their sun-burned thighs.
She looks into their eyes:
can they remember a night
when the stars rose like a host
in the spring sky?

She stares at her abdomen
where beneath the tight skin
a sea churns,
alive with that small fish
whose gills prepare for the barbed air.
A heavy wave pulls her to shore,
drops her amongst the stones

and cracked shells.

Mary Balazs, *The Virago Book of Birth Poetry*, **1993**

• Discuss the images in the poem.

• Write down the thoughts and feelings of this girl, perhaps
  as a diary entry or as a letter to a close friend.

■ MY BABY HAS NO NAME YET
My baby has no name yet;
like a new-born chick or a puppy,
my baby is not named yet.

What numberless texts I examined
at dawn and night and evening over again!
But not one character did I find
which is as lovely as the child.

Starry field of the sky,
or heap of pearls in the depth.
Where can the name be found, how can I?

My baby has no name yet;
like an unnamed bluebird or white flowers
from the furthest land for the first,
I have no name for this baby of ours.

Kim Nam-Jo, translated from the Korean by Ko Won,
The Virago Book of Birth Poetry, **1993**

- Find some music to accompany this poem. Create a dance to go with the poem or, if anyone can sign, set it to sign language.

FURTHER READING

Flour Babies by Anne Fine, Hamish Hamilton, 1992
Teen Scene: Pregnancy by Anne Coates pub. by Wayland 1991
Dear Nobody by Berlie Doherty, HarperCollins Children's Books

AGENCIES AND ADVICE CENTRES

Brook Advisory Centre, 153A East Street, London, SE17 2SD (0207-7039660)

British Pregnancy Advisory Service, 76 Leigham Court Road, London, SW16 2QA (0208-6771241)

National Council For One Parent Families, 255 Kentish Town Road, London NW5 2LX (0207-4285400)

ACKNOWLEDGEMENTS

Tracey Nathan – Sheffield Centre for HIV and Sexual Health and Crucible Theatre in Education.

ACTIVITIES MAPPING

English Framework Objectives (Year 7/8/9)

Page Number	Word (W) & Sentence (S) Level	Learning Objectives (Year 7/8/9)		Speaking & Listening
		Text Level		
		Reading	Writing	
63–5		**(7)** 6, 8		**(7)** 13, 15, 16, 17, 19 **(8)** 14, 15, 16 **(9)** 10, 11, 12, 14
66	**(7)** S15 **(8)** S12		**(7)** 6, 7, 9, 10, 19 **(8)** 5, 10, 18	
70		**(7)** 6	**(7)** 2, 6, 7, 8, 10, 14 **(8)** 5, 6, 7, 10, 12	**(7)** 15, 16 **(9)** 12
71				**(7)** 15, 16, 17, 19 **(8)** 14, 15 **(9)** 12, 14
72		**(7)** 8	**(7)** 5, 6, 7, 9 **(8)** 5	**(7)** 17
74		**(7)** 6, 8	**(7)** 2	**(7)** 15, 16, 17, 18, 19 **(8)** 14, 15, 16 **(9)** 12, 14

Page Number	Word (W) & Sentence (S) Level	Text Level		Speaking & Listening
		Reading	Writing	
		Learning Objectives (Year 7/8/9)		
75				**(7)** 12, 13, 14 **(8)** 10, 12
76			**(7)** 3	**(7)** 12, 13, 14 **(8)** 10, 12
78			**(7)** 1	**(7)** 15, 16, 17, 18 **(8)** 14, 15, 16 **(9)** 3, 12, 14
80		**(7)** 6		**(7)** 12, 13, 14 **(8)** 10, 11, 12
81				**(7)** 12, 14 **(8)** 10
82			**(7)** 9, 17	**(7)** 12, 14, 15, 17 **(8)** 10, 16
85		**(7)** 1, 2, 4, 5	**(7)** 11	
88		**(7)** 1, 2, 4, 5, 6	**(7)** 9	**(7)** 11, 12, 13, 14 **(8)** 10, 11

93				(7) 8 (8) 11 (9) 7	(7) 11, 12, 13, 14, 15, 16, 17, 19 (8) 10, 11, 14, 15, 16 (9) 12, 13, 14
94		(7) 6, 8, 9 (8) 7	(7) 6, 8		
95	(8) W11	(7) 3, 6	(7) 6, 8		(7) 12, 14 (8) 10
96					(7) 15

Other titles in the **Collins** Plays Plus and
Plays Plus Classics series that you might enjoy:

The Tulip Touch

ANNE FINE

A stunning adaptation by the author of
the best-selling novel featuring the story
of a disturbed teenager.
Themes: Juvenile crime; growing up and
friendship
Cast: 22 characters (plus extras)

ISBN 0 00 713086 4

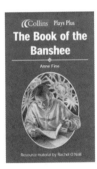

The Book of the Banshee

ANNE FINE

Adapted by Anne Fine from her popular
novel, this is the story of teenage rebellion
and its effects on a family.
Themes: Gender roles; family; growing up;
pacifism and rebellion
Cast: 6 characters

ISBN 0 00 330310 1

Flour Babies

ANNE FINE

The amusing and moving adaptation of
the novel exploring one boy's attempt to
come to terms with his absent father
through a school project on parenting.
Themes: Parenting; family
Cast: 19 characters

ISBN 0 00 330312 8

The Granny Project
ANNE FINE

When Ivan finds himself responsible for looking after his grandmother single-handedly he finds he has more than he had bargained for. The play is a humorous take on family roles and sensitively explores the issue of ageism.

Themes: Ageism; family roles; parenting
Cast: 7 characters

ISBN 0 00 330234 2

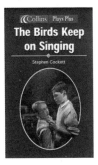

The Birds Keep on Singing
STEPHEN COCKETT

The story of three evacuees billeted with two sisters during World War II. As the adults struggle to cope, the children come to a truce of their own.

Themes: War; relationships
Cast: 11 characters

ISBN 0 00 330315 2

Street Child
BERLIE DOHERTY

Adapted from the award-winning book, *Street Child* is the story of the boy whose plight inspired Dr Barnardo to found his famous children's homes.

Themes: Homelessness; families
Cast: 55 characters (plus extras)

ISBN 0 00 330222 9

Black Harvest
NIGEL GRAY

A tense and gripping drama set on the rugged west coast of Ireland. A fun family holiday goes horribly wrong when the horrors of the Irish potato famine return to haunt them.

Themes: Famine
Cast: 10 characters

ISBN 0 00 330233 4

Mean to be Free

JOANNA HALPERT KRAUS

Set in America's deep south in the 19th century, this is the true story of Harriet Tubman, an ex-slave, who led slaves to freedom in Canada.
Themes: Slavery; freedom
Cast: 15 characters

ISBN 0 00 330240 7

The Thief

JAN NEEDLE

Focusing on a boy falsely accused of stealing, *The Thief* is a stimulating school-based drama.
Themes: Youth crime; self-deception; prejudice
Cast: 20 characters

ISBN 0 00 330237 7

In Holland Stands a House

SUE SAUNDERS

Based on the plight of Anne Frank who, with her family, went into hiding during the Nazi occupation. Drawing on her diary, the play skilfully interweaves domestic scenes from the annexe with wider events happening in Europe.
Themes: The Holocaust; racism; family; relationships
Cast: 11 characters (plus chorus)

ISBN 0 00 330242 3

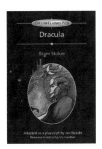

Dracula

BRAM STOKER
(Adapted by Jan Needle)

A blood-sucking count who lives in a
coffin – is this the vision of a madman, or
a terrible truth? This is a dark
dramatisation of Stoker's classic horror
story.
Themes: Gender roles; death
Cast: 14 characters

ISBN 0 00 330224 5

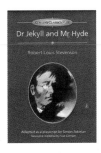

Dr Jekyll and Mr Hyde

ROBERT LOUIS STEVENSON
(Adapted by Simon Adorian)

Presented in the form of a TV
documentary involving expert witnesses
trying to get to the bottom of the mystery
surrounding Dr Jekyll and Mr Hyde, this
dramatisation of Stevenson's classic tale is
ideal for use in schools.
Themes: Drugs; transformation; mental
illness; the media
Cast: 19 characters (plus chorus)

ISBN 0 00 323078 3

The Woman in White

WILKIE COLLINS
(Adapted by Keith West)

Walter and Marian are determined to get to the bottom of the mystery surrounding the woman in white who haunts them, even if it costs them their lives.

Themes: Mental illness; marriage; love
Cast: 13 characters (plus extras)

ISBN 0 00 323077 5

Lorna Doone

R. D. BLACKMORE
(Adapted by Berlie Doherty)

Blackmore's classic tale of high adventure set in the south west of England during the turbulent time of Monmouth's rebellion in 1685.

Themes: Love; class; law
Cast: 28 characters (plus extras)

ISBN 0 00 330226 1